W9-CHK-711

Praise for Pamela Ford's novels

"Ms. Ford has delivered a truly delightful take.
The Sister Switch is definitely headed for
this reviewer's keeper shelf."
—*Romance Readers Connection*

"Ford's writing is strong,
her plot is interesting and the dialogue
between her characters sparkles."
—*Romantic Times BOOKreviews*
on *The Sister Switch*

"A warm-hearted family story,
a sweet, feel-good romance…
a thoroughly enjoyable book."
—*Romance Reviews Today* on *The Sister Switch*

"A humorous story,
filled with romance and down-to-earth
characters that will steal your heart."
—*Cataromance.com* on *Dear Cordelia*

"A whimsical treat."
—*Romantic Times BOOKreviews* on *Oh Baby!*

"Pamela Ford's stories take your heart
on a delightful roller coaster ride
of laughter and tears."
—Ana Leigh, *New York Times*
and *USA TODAY* bestselling author

Dear Reader,

Life has a funny way of pushing us around. Just when we decide to go after what we're sure will make us happy, life throws us a curveball. Only later—sometimes years later—do we realize that getting hit with an unexpected curve was the best thing that ever happened to us.

That's the case with Delaney McBride and Mike Connery. Both know exactly what they want, and it doesn't involve love. Childhood friends who haven't seen one another in fifteen years, they're reunited by Delaney's great-aunt's will and are forced to work together to earn their inheritances.

For Delaney, it's the curveball she never saw coming. Her aunt ran a wedding-planning shop, and Delaney—who doesn't believe in happily ever after—must finish planning the weddings left on the books. Sparks fly in every respect as Mike and Delaney work to meet the terms of the will, only to discover someone else is working just as hard to make sure they fail.

I love hearing from readers. Please let me know what you think of *The Wedding Heiress,* and take a chance at winning one of my giveaways, at www.pamelaford.net.

Pamela

THE WEDDING HEIRESS
Pamela Ford

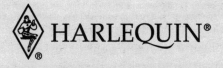

HARLEQUIN®

TORONTO • NEW YORK • LONDON
AMSTERDAM • PARIS • SYDNEY • HAMBURG
STOCKHOLM • ATHENS • TOKYO • MILAN • MADRID
PRAGUE • WARSAW • BUDAPEST • AUCKLAND

If you purchased this book without a cover you should be aware that this book is stolen property. It was reported as "unsold and destroyed" to the publisher, and neither the author nor the publisher has received any payment for this "stripped book."

ISBN-13: 978-0-373-78266-6
ISBN-10:   0-373-78266-7

THE WEDDING HEIRESS

Copyright © 2008 by Pamela Ford.

All rights reserved. Except for use in any review, the reproduction or utilization of this work in whole or in part in any form by any electronic, mechanical or other means, now known or hereafter invented, including xerography, photocopying and recording, or in any information storage or retrieval system, is forbidden without the written permission of the publisher, Harlequin Enterprises Limited, 225 Duncan Mill Road, Don Mills, Ontario, Canada M3B 3K9.

This is a work of fiction. Names, characters, places and incidents are either the product of the author's imagination or are used fictitiously, and any resemblance to actual persons, living or dead, business establishments, events or locales is entirely coincidental.

This edition published by arrangement with Harlequin Books S.A.

® and TM are trademarks of the publisher. Trademarks indicated with ® are registered in the United States Patent and Trademark Office, the Canadian Trade Marks Office and in other countries.

www.eHarlequin.com

Printed in U.S.A.

ABOUT THE AUTHOR

Pamela Ford's first book was a finalist in the Romance Writers of America's prestigious Golden Heart contest for unpublished writers. Since then she has penned three more novels and received a Cataromance Reviewer's Choice Award. Pamela spent many years writing for advertising agencies and corporations before chasing down her dream of becoming a freelance writer and novelist. To reach Pamela, write to her through her Web site at www.pamelaford.net.

Books by Pamela Ford

HARLEQUIN SUPERROMANCE

*Singles…with Kids

Don't miss any of our special offers. Write to us at the following address for information on our newest releases.

Harlequin Reader Service
U.S.: 3010 Walden Ave., P.O. Box 1325, Buffalo, NY 14269
Canadian: P.O. Box 609, Fort Erie, Ont. L2A 5X3

To Bob. They don't come better than you.

ACKNOWLEDGMENTS

My thanks to all the people
who helped give this story life:

Teri Wagner, Jim Casper, Brett Stabelfeldt,
Kate Neugent, Jay Rakowski, Lucy Weller,
Steve Bell at the Division of Health, George Evans
and Karin Wagner at von Briesen & Roper,
Julie Zoellner at Locker's Florist,
Nancy Eschenburg at Milwaukee Lawn Sprinklers,
Police Captain Mark Ferguson, John Kosobucki at
the Wisconsin Board of Bar Examiners
and John Crow at homespy.com.

CHAPTER ONE

DELANEY MCBRIDE knew her fortunes had
changed the moment the telephone rang. She
tap-danced across the room to take the call
she'd been waiting for all afternoon, the one
that would put her back in control of her life.
She paused to compose herself, then said in her
most businesslike voice, "Delaney McBride."

"Pumpkin. How the hell are you?"

Her brain stopped. Her heart stilled.
Suddenly she was the fat, orange-haired
teenager who'd obsessed over Mike Connery
all her life. The high-school junior who'd
pressed a note into Mike's hand that said she
would *save* herself for him. Her face began
to burn. Thank God she and her mother had
moved out of town a few months later.

"Pumpkin?"

She dropped into the soft leather cushion
of her living-room sofa and pressed a hand to
her cheek, the heat warming her palm. How

could something she did fifteen years ago have such an effect on her today? This call was supposed to be a job offer, not a connection to a past she'd rather forget. She tried to pull her thoughts into order. "Yes?"

"This is Mike Connery from—"

"Holiday Bay. I know." The words came out more sharply than she intended. Surely he wasn't calling about the will.

"I'm sorry about your great-aunt. She was a wonderful lady."

A sympathy call from Mike Connery? "Thanks. She was really special."

"Uh, I'm calling about her will."

There it was. She exhaled. Well, why *wouldn't* he call? He stood to lose as much as anyone else. For a moment, she felt a certain camaraderie with him, swept like everyone else into the maelstrom of her aunt's eccentricity by the woman's last will.

She shoved her bangs off her forehead as if to shove the emotion away. "I can't believe this will is legal," she said. "I've never heard of anything so absurd. I even met with another lawyer…"

"I'm an attorney, Pumpy. It's ironclad."

Her stomach tightened. She wasn't Pumpy

anymore. Pumpkin and her insecurities no longer existed, thanks to years of therapy. She wanted to tell Mike to call her Delaney, but couldn't bring herself to let on that the nickname bothered her. She made a fist, then let out a controlled laugh. "So my attorney confirmed," she said in a low voice. "Although, as a lawyer you should know nothing is ever ironclad if you have the right connections."

He gave an equally controlled chuckle. "Does that mean we shouldn't count on you? I'll tell the other heirs so they can quit planning…"

"Planning?"

"Yeah… To pay off credit cards, take their first vacation in years, have an operation. Sully Sullivan was going back to Ireland to see his mother. Hasn't seen her in twenty-five years, and she's getting old."

"Is this why you're calling? To pressure me into complying with that ridiculous will? To guilt me into overseeing a bunch of weddings?" Delaney stood and crossed the living room of her Victorian row house to look out at the organic food store across the street. She'd chosen to live in Boston's South End because it was full of young professionals, people with drive and an eye on the future.

Her lifestyle was totally incongruous with wedding planning.

He ignored her questions. "Are you in or not?"

God knew she needed the hundred thousand dollars her great-aunt had left her. She'd been unemployed for more than three months, laid off when the ad agency where she worked lost her big account. Now she was in debt up to her eyeballs. Her savings were depleted, her rent was due, her car payment was overdue, the balance on her credit card kept going up, and all she had to live on was a small unemployment check. The mere thought of her finances made her heart begin to race and she sucked in a breath to calm herself.

"Pumpkin?"

Which made this inheritance a godsend. Except, in order to get the money, which she desperately needed, she had to go to back to her hometown in Wisconsin—Holiday Bay. Worse, she had to finish planning the weddings that remained on the books of her late aunt's shop.

"Are you in or out?" he pressed.

"It's not that simple."

"What's the problem? You have an aversion to money?" he said with thinly disguised impatience.

She huffed. She was supposed to be getting a job offer today. One with a salary that would nearly rival what she'd receive from her inheritance—and wouldn't require she plan weddings to get paid. If only she'd heard from them already. "Of course not. It's just, I'm not sure I have the time to take this on. I don't know a thing about wedding planning."

"You don't have to be incredible at it, just good enough to—"

"And frankly, I'm not into that happily-ever-after scene."

Mike laughed out loud. "Seems to me you were quite the little hopeless romantic in your day."

Every possible thought in her head vaporized. For a moment she couldn't speak. What kind of man would bring up her old infatuation with him to win an argument? She forced herself to say something, anything. "Yes, well, I've long since learned the error of my ways."

He made a choking sound. "So you'd give up one hundred thousand dollars because you don't want to plan a few weddings? Hell, for one hundred thousand dollars, I'd clean out horse stalls bare-handed. And I'd smile the whole time."

"Therein lies the difference between us, now, doesn't it," she said with a sniff.

"We're talking about a few months, not a lifetime. So what is it really? You don't need the money? You can't get a leave from your job?"

"I can take off whenever I want." With no job at all, taking time off wasn't an issue, but she just didn't feel like baring her entire life to him. She'd already spent enough years being a loser in Mike Connery's eyes. She opened the front door and stepped outside, pausing at the top of the steep concrete steps. A cool spring breeze slid over her bare arms.

"What's the big deal, then? You afraid to fail? Or afraid to try?"

"I just told you."

He laughed out loud, a long laugh that took her straight back to high school. It irritated her to no end. They were talking to each other with the same friendly antagonism they'd had in childhood, as though fifteen years hadn't even passed.

"I get it. You've got a boyfriend."

"No, I don't."

"You're so in love you don't want to leave Boston."

"You're full of crap." Her voice went up a notch and she grasped the stair rail. God, he was the same old Mike. A year older than she and always had to win the arguments. Didn't matter if the sky was blue; he'd argue that it was pink until he won. No wonder he'd become a lawyer.

She heard a call-waiting beep and pulled the phone away from her ear to check the caller ID screen. It was the ad agency she'd been waiting to hear from. *With her job offer.* She grinned. No wedding planning in her future.

"I have to call you back. I've got a business call on the other line." She clicked him off without waiting for a reply.

Mike was so wrong. No boyfriend would ever prevent her from doing something she wanted to do. That described her mother— and she would never be like her mother. Always needing a man to rely on, always thinking a man would make everything better. Then never getting the man.

Ten minutes later she felt more like her mother than she ever had in her life. All dressed up and nowhere to go. Reaching for the brass ring and missing once again. She stared out her front windows without seeing a thing. They'd offered the job to someone else.

Someone with more experience. When all was said and done, she hadn't been good enough.

She glanced at her watch without knowing why. She had no place she needed to be, no meetings, no conference calls, no deadlines. She wanted to bang her head against a wall. How could she have lost complete control of her life? She had no job. She had no money. She had no prospects. *She had no choices.* None except go to Holiday Bay and get up to her elbows in white satin, butter-cream frosting and rosebud bouquets. She loved her aunt dearly, but what had ever made the woman think this was a good plan?

"I can't do it, I can't go back there," she said to no one, knowing full well that was exactly what she had to do—at least until a high-paying job offer came her way.

She knew she should call Mike back, but decided to put it off for a while. She thought about him and wondered whether his teenage good looks had matured into handsome. Whether he was still as lean and fit as when he was playing high-school baseball. Whether his black hair was prematurely peppered with white like his father's had been. And whether his blue eyes could still make her heart pound.

Afraid? Darn right she was afraid. But it wasn't wedding planning she was afraid of.

MIKE ROUNDED THE DOOR of his law office to find his friend, Dan Hobart, kicked back in the black leather desk chair, work boots up on the cherrywood desk and fingers laced behind his head. Though his blue mechanic's jumpsuit looked completely out of place in the richly appointed office, Dan's demeanor was that of a full partner. Mike leaned against the doorway and grinned. "Anything I can get to make you more comfortable, Hobes?" he asked.

"How about a massage therapist?" Dan grinned, then pulled his feet off the desk and sat up. "I had to drop Bill Brighton's car off for him and figured I'd stop in before I head back to the shop. Did you talk to Pumpkin?"

Mike nodded. "You know how she used to be the tagalong, the gnat we were always trying to get rid of? Well, now she's morphed into a giant pain-in-the-ass."

"Still a no-go, huh?"

"Yeah. She's going to call me back, but I'm not holding out a lot of hope," he said.

"We should have left her tied to that maple tree when she was eight."

Despite his irritation, Mike laughed. He

could still see chubby Pumpkin McBride with her mop of unruly orange hair as they ditched her in the woods with the false assurance that this was how you played King Arthur and they'd be back for her in five minutes. Three hours later, it had taken a Hershey bar and the seventy-two cents they'd pooled between them to keep her from tattling. "Could be she wants revenge because I hit her with an arrow that time we were playing William Tell," he said.

"It was only a foam arrow," Dan said. "I can't believe she'd hold that against you."

"I suspect her memory may be long."

Dan started to chortle. "Maybe she didn't like that snowman we made in her front yard—the one where we put a real pumpkin on the top for a head." He sobered. "So what do you think's the problem?"

"I don't know." Mike shoved his hands in the pockets of his khakis. "Maybe she doesn't need the money."

"Doesn't she care that the rest of us do?" Dan took a drink from his coffee cup and grimaced. "Cold."

"Doesn't sound like it. I played all the guilt cards. Even told her Sully wanted to go back to Ireland to see his mother."

Dan snorted. "You nabbed the plot from *Going My Way?* What if she's seen the movie?"

"It was a spur-of-the-moment strategy. I just couldn't believe anyone would seriously consider giving up one hundred thousand dollars no matter what clause was attached to it." He collapsed into one of the upholstered chairs opposite his desk.

"She knows she's not the only heir that has to do something, doesn't she?" Dan asked. "That we have to restore the '57 Chevy. That other people have to—"

"She got a copy of the will."

Dan stood and walked across the office, turning to face Mike. "The way I see it, you only have one choice."

"Me?"

"Yeah, you. She was always in love with you."

Mike laughed. "Not anymore."

"You can get it back—women never forget their first loves. Play to that attraction and you'll get her to sign on. Once she's knee-deep in wedding planning, you can slide away, no one the wiser. Then we can all get our inheritances and live happily ever after."

"I've got news for you. She's not into that

happily-ever-after scene," Mike said, standing. "Her words. Not mine."

Dan clapped him on the back. "Well, then, you're just the man to change her mind."

The office phone rang and Dan leaned over and picked it up after one ring. "Connery Law Office. How can we help you?" he said cheerfully. His eyes narrowed as he asked, "May I tell him who's calling?" One hand over the mouthpiece, he raised his eyebrows at Mike and whispered, "Pumpkin. Be nice. *Really* nice."

Mike put the phone to his ear and sat on the edge of the desk. "Hey, Pumpkin, thanks for calling back," he said in the friendliest voice he could muster. "Dan and I were just talking about all the fun we three had as kids."

Dan rolled his eyes.

Silence greeted him from the other end of the line. Maybe he'd gone too far. "Pumpy?"

"Okay," she said. "I've, ah, thought the whole thing over and decided to, ah…that it would be worthwhile for me to give wedding planning a try. Do one or two weddings and—"

"That's great!"

"So I cleared my schedule for a couple of weeks."

"Everyone will be happy to hear this." Mike gave Dan a thumbs-up.

Dan jabbed an index finger in the air. "Play it up," he whispered.

"*I'm* happy to hear this," Mike added hastily. "Can't wait to see you. When will you get here?"

"I'm driving, so it'll be a few days. Is Sunday soon enough?" she asked less than enthusiastically.

Dan did a little hip-hop dance around the room, his fingers curled in the symbol for "rock on." Mike ignored him. "The first wedding is less than two weeks away, so I guess the sooner the better. I'll have someone open the apartment above your great-aunt's wedding shop so it'll be ready for you to move in."

"Thanks. Um, guess I'll see you next week."

"I'm looking forward to it." Yeah, right. What he was looking forward to was getting this whole thing out of the way and his life returning to normal. He hung up the phone and pointed at his friend. "Houston, we have liftoff. She's going to try a wedding or two."

Dan froze. "*Try* it? She's got to do the whole job."

"One step at a time. At least she's coming to town."

"Yeah, but none of us gets our inheritances unless everyone fulfills the terms of the will. If we lose Pumpkin, we all lose."

"We won't lose her."

"There's only one way to be sure of that." Dan smirked at Mike like the Cheshire cat.

"Oh, no. Don't look at me."

"Oh, yes. It's only for a couple of months. You don't have to seduce her. Just keep our sweet Pumpkin happy so she doesn't quit before all the weddings are finished."

Mike gaped at Dan for a long moment, then dropped down into the chair, shaking his head. As much as he didn't want to do it, he had to admit Dan was right. For everyone to get their inheritance, he had to make Pumpy his own personal project over the next couple of months.

CHAPTER TWO

DELANEY WALKED SLOWLY across the worn hardwood floor of Ellie Clark's Storybook Weddings shop. She had never seen so much white in one place in all her life. White satin, white lace, white netting, white garters, shoes, stockings, candles, favors, guest books... Argh. Everywhere she turned it was white, white, white, white, white.

And for what? The pursuit of the everlasting fairy tale? Had anyone ever bothered to ask Cinderella how she liked living with her in-laws five years after the wedding? Or whether Snow White still awoke with a smile from Prince Charming's kisses?

Storybook weddings indeed!

She glanced at Megan Hobart, standing at the work counter, one hand resting on her very pregnant belly, the other flipping through the pages of a big ledger. With her blond ponytail and quick smile, Megan was as cute today as she had been in high school.

Megan grinned for about the tenth time in ten minutes. "I'm so happy you're here. Even when Mike told us you were coming, I was afraid you'd change your mind at the last minute. Say you didn't need the money or something."

Not need one hundred thousand dollars? Hardly. Delaney picked up a clear glass slipper from the shelf and peered through it at eye level. Who bought this stuff?

Dumb question. The cottage crowd, of course, though, you'd be hard-pressed to call those lake homes *cottages* anymore. The only reason such an unusual wedding shop could survive so far away from a major metropolitan area was that Holiday Bay drew so many vacationers. Like the rest of the towns in Door County, the downtown was filled with quaint boutiques, antique stores and fudge shops. All of which added to its charm and made it a favorite place for weddings of the adult children of the cottage owners.

She set the slipper back on the shelf and ran a hand down a swath of white satin. Five weddings. She had to finish the planning and execution of the last five May and June weddings before she could get her inheritance. Though she'd told Mike she was just going to give it a try, the truth was she had no other options.

Self-doubt filled her, a rather common occurrence ever since she'd received the call about the inheritance from her great-uncle Lou, Ellie's brother. "I still don't understand why Aunt Ellie wrote such an unusual will," she said to Megan. "I don't know a thing about planning weddings. This weekend could be a disaster in the making."

"That's pretty unlikely. Ellie took care of most things already—catering, flowers, the band, alterations." Megan ran a finger down the open ledger, then looked up at Delaney. "All you need to do is make sure everything happens on Saturday when it's supposed to. Your aunt was totally organized."

Delaney moved to stand beside Megan and scan the page. Names, phone numbers, contacts, details, you name it, it was all there. She bit her lower lip. She'd never run from a challenge before. As long as she applied the principles of effective management she should be able to pull this off.

Probably. Maybe. Perhaps.

"I'm so glad you're here," Megan said.

"For a while I thought I was going to have to make these weddings happen—with a two-year-old at home and a baby due in a couple of weeks, and a doctor who keeps telling me to take it easy. Like that's possible with Kristian, anyway. I swear he has more energy than any toddler I've ever seen."

"Thank God Aunt Ellie didn't schedule a wedding every weekend." Otherwise Delaney thought she might have a mental breakdown right now. "I just don't get it. Why am I here?"

"Because you want to make sure five couples are able to enter wedded bliss in the most romantic way possible."

Delaney controlled the urge to roll her eyes. "No."

Megan closed the book and tilted her head thoughtfully. "Because you love the idea of making fairy tales come true—white doves, white horses, white swans—"

"No." The horror of her situation began to sink in. White doves and swans? Glass slippers? Golden carriages? She was actually going to do this?

"Hmm." Megan stared at her for a long moment, then scrunched up her face. "Well, there's always the inheritance."

Delaney grinned.

"You're only doing this for the money?" Megan's brow furrowed.

"Well, yeah. Why else would I do it?"

"To help people make their big day one they'll never forget. To send them out into their new lives surrounded by magic." She opened her arms wide. "I just love this shop."

Oh, God, Megan was one of those romantics. Delaney brushed her shoulder-length hair behind her ear. What exquisite irony. She, the one in charge, was doing this strictly for an inheritance. Her assistant was the googly eyed romantic.

"You know what I think?" Megan lifted a spangle-studded wedding tiara off a display, set it on her head and fluffed the attached veil over her shoulders. She spun in a circle. "I think that once you've done a couple of weddings, you'll find romance has gotten into your heart and under your skin. You'll want to give up advertising for the enchanted world of fairy-tale wedding planning."

Delaney shook her head. Hopeless. Absolutely hopeless. It was going to be a long couple of months.

Megan snatched up a bouquet of blush-and-cream silk roses and thrust it into

Delaney's hands. "Hold this a minute." Then she pulled the tiara off her own head and plopped it onto Delaney's, smoothing the waist-length veil down the back. She clasped her hands together. "With your red hair you could be a model!" She turned Delaney toward the wall mirror. "Now, doesn't that make you feel even a bit roman—"

A bell tinkled at the front door and two handsome thirtysomething men stepped inside, both wearing dirty jeans and sweatshirts, both carrying themselves with the easy self-assurance of athletes.

"You remember Dan and Mike, don't you?" Megan danced across the shop floor to share a quick kiss with the taller of the two, the one who was obviously her husband, Dan. It had been fifteen years since Delaney had seen either of the men. As memories of adolescence began to crowd her mind, she purposely focused her attention on Dan. Though he was over six feet tall and more than a few pounds heavier since high school, he still had the same impish grin and, no doubt, the same mischievous personality.

"Is this our new wedding planner?" Mike asked.

Delaney finally let herself look at him.

Mike Connery. Shorter than Dan, but still lean and fit, his jaw still strong and, yeah, just as she'd suspected, streaks of silver in his black hair.

"This is her!" Megan gestured expressively.

Only then did Delaney remember the veil. She snatched the thing off her head, her eyes locking with Mike's just long enough for a sigh to catch in her throat. Damn, but those blue eyes could still wrap her in their spell. She crumpled the veil in her fist.

MIKE TRIED TO HIDE his shock. This was Pumpkin? Little, round, red-haired pumpkin was now... Hell, in her tight jeans and a clingy T-shirt, it was easy to see they'd never be calling her Plumpy Pumpy again.

"Welcome back!" Dan hugged her. "You look great. Mike, doesn't she look great?"

"Yeah. I almost didn't recognize you," he said. He had to admit, he had excellent conversational skills. He could feel Dan's hand in the small of his back propelling him toward Pumpkin. He took a step forward and gave her a hug. After a second, she broke the contact.

"Hi, Mike. Dan. Nice to see you again."

"So what are you two boys doing here in

the middle of the day? Don't you have cars to fix?" Megan asked.

"We wanted to say hi to Pumpkin," Dan said.

Cars to fix? They were still working on cars? She frowned at Mike. "I thought you were a lawyer."

"Lawyer. Mechanic. What's the difference?" Dan smiled. "They both make the world go round."

Delaney looked from one to the other. "Seriously, what do you guys do?"

"We're mechanics," Mike said just as Dan said, "We're lawyers."

"Stop it, you two." Megan slapped Dan's arm. "Mike's a lawyer. Dan took over his dad's shop when he retired a couple of years ago."

"I'm not just a pretty boy," Mike added. "I'm a mechanic, too."

Delaney looked at Dan, her brow furrowed.

"He was hanging around the shop so much when he moved back to town, I took pity on him and gave him a job," Dan explained.

"Pity? You couldn't find help as good with cars as I am."

"Part-time," Dan said. "Really part-time. It makes him feel useful."

Mike grinned. "We just moved your aunt's

'57 Chevy into the shop and I was checking it over to see what needs fixing."

"They've been coveting that car forever," Megan said. "Now they're like two kids who've taken over the candy store."

"Once we get it running, Mike'll take you for a drive," Dan said.

Mike cleared his throat. No master of subtlety, Dan. "We actually did stop by to talk about something other than cars," he said. "Since all the heirs have to succeed for any of us to inherit, we want to hold regular meetings. Once a week until the deadline."

"Follow each other's progress. Cheer each other on. Listen to tapes of motivational speakers," Dan said.

Delaney's hazel eyes widened.

"It's best to ignore him most of the time," Mike said. "Makes life easier. Anyway, we're thinking of holding the first one tomorrow night at seven. In the public meeting room at the library."

"Do you really think we need it?" Delaney asked.

For a moment no one said anything, as surprised as he was, Mike figured, that she didn't outright agree. The Pumpkin he used to know would have just gone along.

"Well, it's a nice way to support each other. And you can meet all the heirs," Megan offered.

"But I just got into town and—"

"Monday's the only night that worked for everyone," Dan said.

"I'm not sure about taking the time. I'll have a lot to do before Saturday's—"

"Your aunt has this wedding pretty well organized," Megan said.

Delaney shook her head. "I don't know. It just seems sort of unnecessary. I mean, isn't the money motivation enough for everyone?"

Obviously not for her, Mike thought. Pumpkin's lack of commitment was the main reason they'd decided to hold heirs' meetings. "Even if you don't need it, I think it would be helpful to the rest of us," Mike said. "To keep everyone committed."

Delaney looked at him with an expression he couldn't read. The Pumpkin of old had never been able to hide her feelings about anything. Her face always gave her away and her heart had always been on her sleeve.

"I guess we can try one meeting," she finally said.

Try. There was that word again. Dan caught his eye and nodded almost imperceptibly. Mike knew exactly what his friend was saying—it was time to kick the Pumpkin Project into high gear.

DELANEY KEPT THINKING about the conversation long after Mike and Dan had gone. She'd come to town hoping she could just quietly give the weddings a shot and then leave. She didn't want to get involved here and especially didn't want Mike to think she'd spent years pining for him.

Because she hadn't. But the moment she'd set eyes on him in the wedding shop, she realized how easily she could become attracted to him again. And she was in no mood for unattainable adolescent fantasies. Which was why she hadn't wanted to go to the heirs' meeting. As silly as it sounded, she knew the less time she spent around Mike the better off she'd be. She sighed. Fine, she would go. But she'd be the last one in the door and the first one out.

MONDAY NIGHT AT SEVEN o'clock, Mike took a seat at the old hardwood conference table in the library meeting room with the rest of Ellie Clark's heirs. Reality smacked him in the face. Every person in this small group had to accomplish the task they were assigned in the will. Damn, but was this going to be one hell of an undertaking. He'd listed the heirs and each of their assignments on the whiteboard hanging on the wall behind him, but other than having the executor distribute a checklist and talk about what would constitute success—especially with regard to the weddings—he had no real agenda.

Henry "Sully" Sullivan and Henry "Stonewall" Jackson were sitting across from one another, arms crossed over their chests, not speaking. The men, both in their early seventies, had played in a trio with Henry Clark for many years. Now, the two remaining Henrys had to oversee the building of a new band shell at the park, the cost of which would be covered by funds Ellie had earmarked for that purpose. Then the two had to put together a summer Friday-night concert series called Music in the Park—and be the opening act for the first concert.

"How're you guys doing tonight?" Mike asked.

They answered with unintelligible grunts.

Not good. Not good at all. Though their common first name brought the three Henrys together years ago, Sully and Stonewall had always been like oil and vinegar. Henry Clark had been the stabilizing force, the one who was able to keep the peace. Once he died, the other two had drifted apart. Mike ran a hand through his hair. Somehow, these two had to set aside their differences long enough to get the job done.

He and Dan probably had the easiest task—restoring Henry Clark's old Chevy and driving it in the Fourth of July parade. If all went well, they would get the title to the car and fifty thousand dollars each.

"It's past seven," Dan said from his seat next to Megan. "And no Pumpkin."

Mike glanced at his watch. He hoped Pumpkin hadn't changed her mind about coming tonight. He was sure she would become more vested in the outcome if she made a personal connection with the rest of the heirs. "Let's give her a little more time. Maybe she's just running late."

After another five minutes he gave up. "I guess we might as well get started. You all know Ed Snyder." He gestured at a stout middle-aged man sitting at the end of the table. "I asked him to come tonight because he was Ellie's lawyer and he's the executor."

"I've never liked that term." Stonewall pulled on one of his long gray eyebrows. "Sounds like he's supposed to kill people."

"Maybe he could start with you," Sully muttered.

Mike studied the two silver-haired men. "Now, guys—"

"Actually, *executor* isn't used much anymore. The term is usually *personal representative,*" Ed said.

Stonewall let out a snort. "That's like calling a janitor a sanitary engineer."

"There's no law that says we have to use either of those titles. We can call him anything we want," Megan said helpfully.

"That's right," Sully said. "How about we compromise on something like…*will checker?*"

"Will checker? Will checker? Sounds like someone's name." Stonewall extended a hand. "Damn glad to meet you, my name's Will Checker."

"Sometimes you are such a stupid old fool," Sully retorted, his double chin vibrating. "Fine, then you come up with something better."

"I will!" Stonewall pushed back his chair and stood.

The executor held up a hand like a stop sign. "I really think *personal representative* says exactly what—"

"Heir overseer," Stonewall said.

Sully stood. "Heir manager."

Mike threw an exasperated look at Megan and Dan, both of whom were obviously holding in laughter. "How about heir patrol?" Dan said, smirking.

Both Henrys nodded. "I like it," Sully said.

"And our slogan could be…" a woman's voice said from the doorway.

Mike turned to see Pumpkin step into the room, her red hair curling softly around her face, her hazel eyes full of laughter.

"Our slogan could be," she repeated, "heir-ly to bed and heir-ly to rise makes a man healthy, wealthy and wise. Seems appropriate."

Mike stood. "This, everyone, is our new wedding planner—"

"Delaney McBride," Megan chimed in. "Delaney, these are the Henrys and the execu—personal rep—the guy who's going to oversee the will." Megan introduced each man by name and Pumpkin shook their hands before taking a seat.

Stonewall frowned and sat down. "Let's not get carried away here. We don't need a slogan."

"Heir patrol is enough." Sully sat down, too.

"Let's get on with this," Stonewall said. "We don't have all night to sit around here jawing."

Mike held himself back from pointing out to Stonewall that he was the one who started this inane discussion.

"Sorry I'm late," Delaney said. "I just got off a long conversation with a bride about whether she should have the guests throw confetti or rice after the ceremony."

"What did she decide?" Megan asked.

"Confetti. Turquoise and peach to go with her exotic island theme."

Mike cleared his throat. "Ladies?" Once he had everyone's attention he began again. "Since we all have to meet the terms of the will to inherit, Ed brought some forms."

The executor held up a bunch of papers.

"Don't we need to vote on 'heir patrol'?" Sully asked.

Whatever. "All in favor of 'heir patrol' say *aye.*"

"You're not following Robert's Rules of Order," Stonewall said.

"I don't think we need to be so formal," Ed said.

"Maybe we should vote on it." Delaney smiled sweetly at Mike and crossed her long legs.

Mike forced a smile. "All in favor of Robert's Rules of Order, say *aye.*"

Stonewall's lone *aye* echoed in the large room.

"All opposed say *nay*," Mike said, in proper Robert's Rules format.

A chorus of *nays* rang out.

One battle over. Now to get rid of "heir patrol" just as quickly. "All in favor of 'heir patrol,' say aye," he said.

The two Henrys and Pumpkin chorused aye.

"The motion passes," he said.

"There wasn't a motion," Stonewall pointed out.

Enough was enough. "Ed Snyder is officially the heir patrol. Is it all right with everyone if we get down to business now?"

Stonewall raised his hand. "How are you two doing on that car? Henry and Ellie left it sitting on the tires for years. I'm sure it can't be driven. You think you'll be finished in eight weeks? Well, seven weeks now."

Dan scrunched up his face in concentration. "We've already ordered all the parts we need," he said. "It'll be tight, but, yeah, come hell or high water, we'll meet the deadline. You don't have to worry about me and Mike."

"I'll second that," Mike said.

"And how about the wedding planning?"

Stonewall focused his attention on Pumpkin. "There's a wedding this weekend."

She frowned. "Fine. I guess. Just trying to figure out all the pieces."

"We've already had another customer!" Megan interjected.

"Who we can't possibly take on," Pumpkin added. "We're not in business to get more business. Anyway, it appears that Aunt Ellie had things well organized, so this wedding should be okay."

"Okay?" Megan chirped. "More than okay! It will be absolutely lovely, a celebration of love to be remembered for a lifetime."

Pumpkin turned slowly to stare at Megan. "Yeah. That."

Mike pointed at the Henrys. "Okay, guys, you're on. How's the new band shell coming along?"

"That deadline is for the birds. We'll never make it," Stonewall said.

Sully glared at him. "Is the glass ever half-full in that godforsaken life of yours?"

Stonewall rubbed a hand across his jaw. "I'm a realist. Any idiot with a brain is going to know we won't be able to have a new band shell built by the Fourth of July."

"They could do it on TV in a week," Sully said.

"Reality shows with hundreds of workers—"

"Failure isn't an option, guys," Mike said. "What can we do to help?"

"We don't need help," Stonewall said. "We need time."

"We're doing okay." Sully struggled to his feet. "Stonewall, sometimes you are such a…"

Stonewall stood and faced his old friend. "Yeah? A what?"

"A—a—boob."

Stonewall's face flushed dark red.

The executor scratched some notes on his yellow legal pad. "There's no reason for anyone to get worked up," he said.

Mike quickly picked up the photocopied forms the man had brought with him and began to pass them out. "Ellie left a list of requirements and a checklist for us to use as we complete our tasks. Listen up, gentlemen, we have way too much to do to be getting into it tonight."

"I'm not getting into anything," Stonewall said. "I'm just stating facts."

"Facts, facts," Sully retorted in a raised

voice. "You always spin the facts to make your point of view look better."

"Are you calling me a liar?"

"You mean you think you're not?"

"That's it!" Stonewall clenched his hands into fists and advanced around the table toward Sully.

"Okay, guys, hold on here." Mike lunged out of his seat at the men. Maybe holding meetings wasn't such a good idea, after all. These two and their antics wouldn't elicit sympathy from Pumpkin; instead, they'd make her think that getting the inheritance would be next to impossible.

"This isn't worth an argument." Pumpkin jumped up and grabbed Stonewall's forearm just as he let loose with a left hook that flung her right along with his fist.

CHAPTER THREE

MIKE WATCHED DELANEY fall as if she were in slow motion; he couldn't move fast enough to help her. This wasn't happening. The heirs weren't really exchanging blows in the local library. Delaney stuck her hands out in front of her to break her fall and landed with a thud on the thinly carpeted floor. Mike could almost feel the impact reverberate up her arms. She lay still for a second, then moaned and sat up, gingerly holding out her left arm.

He knelt beside her. "You okay?"

"I don't know. My wrist…"

"Oh, Pumpkin, I'm so sorry," Stonewall said.

She blinked. "Pumpkin?"

"Isn't that what they call you?"

"Some people do." She glared at Mike.

"Maybe she better go to the hospital," Megan said.

"I'll be fine. Just need some ice." She

twisted her wrist to demonstrate how fine she was and grimaced in pain.

Mike gently prodded the skin around her wrist. "Does that—"

A breath hissed out from between her clenched teeth. "No."

"Liar." Mike shook his head and admired her stupid bravery. "It's swollen already. You're going to the doctor."

"It's not broken."

"How do you know? You get a medical degree since this morning?" He looked up at everyone bending over them. "Meeting adjourned. I'll take Delaney in. The rest of you go home and write one hundred times, *I will get along with my fellow heirs for the next eight weeks.* We'll reconvene next Monday night. Make sure you take a copy of that paper I was handing out *and read it.*"

"I can't come Monday." Sully rested his hands on his T-shirted belly.

"We can't, either." Megan slid her arm through Dan's. "We're touring the birthing center at the hospital."

"Tuesday's out for me," Stonewall said.

"Don't forget, we have a game Wednesday night," Dan said.

Mike helped Pumpkin to her feet. "Fine.

We'll make it Thursday, then. Same time, same place."

Half an hour later, he and Delaney were seated in the emergency waiting room. *Emergency waiting*—an oxymoron if he'd ever heard one.

He eyed Pumpkin for obvious signs of pain. Her wrist appeared even more swollen. "Still hurt?"

She nodded.

Damn. He'd been hoping this was just a minor—temporary—injury.

"What were you doing trying to jump between two men about to have a fistfight?" he asked irritably.

"If you had kept control of those lunatics, I wouldn't have had to jump anywhere. And what's wrong with you, anyway?" Delaney asked. "I'm the one with the broken wrist."

He put an arm around her shoulder. "Maybe it's not broken."

"I believe that's what I said when it happened."

"Hopefully this won't make it too hard for you to do the weddings."

Delaney gave a sharp laugh. "I think I can rely on Megan to make sure every wedding is a fantasy come true."

"Yeah, well, speaking of fantasies come true… Remember that paper I was handing out from the executor when you were—"

"Thrown to the ground? Yes."

He winced. "It was an evaluation form your aunt put together for the brides to fill out after each wedding. There are some fifteen categories they're supposed to rate either 'satisfactory' or 'unsatisfactory.'"

"You've got to be kidding me. Like what? Cake? Band? Favors?"

"Uh-huh. And organization, friendliness of staff, availability of the wedding planner… Each category is worth a certain number of points and the final score determines whether the wedding was satisfactorily completed or not."

Delaney's mouth dropped open. "Give me a break. This job is just one delightful surprise after another. Speaking of surprises, what's the deal with those Henrys? They'll be the downfall of us all."

"They're the reason Dan and I wanted to hold the meetings," Mike lied. He quickly filled her in on the Henrys' history. "We don't want them to forget how many people are relying on them. Maybe they'll be able to put aside their differences until this thing is over."

Delaney sighed and got up. "If that's even possible. I'll be right back. I need a drink of water."

A minute later, the front-desk nurse was bending over him with a clipboard. "Mr. McBride, I need your wife to sign these papers, then we'll take her back to an exam room."

Mr. McBride? Disconcerted, Mike took the clipboard. "She's not— We're not— She's getting a drink."

"When she gets back, just have her sign where I put the red x's, then bring this up to the desk," the nurse said briskly. She headed toward the check-in station.

"Will do," Mike said to her back.

The nurse spotted Delaney returning to the waiting room and waved. "Mrs. McBride," she called, "I gave your husband some papers for you to sign. Then we're ready for you."

Pumpkin stopped in her tracks and looked over at Mike, then back to the nurse. By the time she reached him, she was grinning. "Honey," she said, "you forgot my birthday again."

He found himself mesmerized by the sparkle in her hazel-green eyes. "Yeah? Well, you suck at remembering our anniversary."

She took the clipboard from him. "Obviously the bloom has gone off the rose."

Mike threw back his head and laughed. Pumpkin McBride was nobody's tagalong anymore.

AN HOUR LATER, back at her apartment above Storybook Weddings, Delaney slouched into the worn sofa and flipped through *Money* magazine. Mike had been a good friend tonight, comfortable to be with. It was nice to be in this new place with him. "Those Henrys, on the other hand, are going to be trouble," she muttered.

As nice as the two men might be individually, together they were a screeching, out-of-tune duet. "They'd better do their part. Much as I loved you, Aunt Ellie, I'm not going through wedding-planning hell for nothing."

She pitched the magazine onto the glass-topped coffee table. The problem was, no one seemed to know how to get the Henrys to play nicely together. Not the executor. Not Dan. Not Mike.

She rubbed her wrist, now wrapped in a polyester brace with velcro straps, her fingers sticking out like little sausages. Not broken, the doctor said, just a sprain. She should be happy about that, but even a sprain meant she would be one-handed for a couple of weeks.

She'd come to Holiday Bay intending to stay uninvolved. Yet, two days in town and already she'd jumped into the fray. She closed her eyes.

She needed to talk to someone with more insight into the two Henrys than Mike, someone who'd known them for a long time.

And who better than Ellie's brother, Great-uncle Lou?

She cringed. She'd put off stopping over to say hi because she'd never known Lou well when she lived here, not like she'd known Ellie. As a child, she'd been afraid of him. He was physically imposing, which in itself shouldn't have been a problem. But he'd been so serious all the time, so focused on making money, he never seemed to have any fun. Heck, he'd never even married. Her mother said it was because his family lost everything during the depression and he grew up determined never to be poor again. All Delaney knew was that he spent nearly every minute working.

Still, she wasn't a kid anymore. And she doubted her uncle was the ogre she'd imagined him to be when she was a child. After spending all his seventy years in Holiday Bay, Uncle Lou surely knew something more about the Henrys. Tomorrow she would pay him a visit and see what she could learn.

IT WAS PAST NINE when Mike stepped across the living room and followed the sound of pop music to where his eleven-year-old daughter, Andrea, was dancing in front of the full-length mirror at the end of the hall. She should be in bed by now. He hated having his mother babysit because she had no backbone as far as Andy was concerned. His daughter tossed her light brown hair and sang along with the song. When she spotted his reflection, she spun to face him, glaring, her embarrassment at being caught evident in the pink of her cheeks. She shut off the CD player on the floor. "Dad! What?"

"Where's Grandma?"

"In the basement doing the wash."

No matter how often he told his mother not to, every time she came over she did the laundry. She said it made her feel useful. Drove him nuts.

"Homework done?" he asked.

Andy's expression grew defensive. "Almost."

His stomach tensed at the argument he knew lay ahead. "Andy, I thought we agreed that—"

"Dad, those teachers are *crazy*. They don't think we have lives other than school. I have a life! I have other things to do than homework. Why do they give us so much? And that Mr. Tory, he can't teach math. No one in the class knows what they're doing and—"

"This is just what happens when you get older. Responsibility increases and so does homework."

"I hate middle school."

He was beginning to hate it, too. Especially the melodrama.

"Only a couple more weeks and school's out for the summer. How much homework have you got left?"

"Some math problems. And I have to make a poster showing different types of energy. Do we have any bristol board?"

"Is this thing due tomorrow?"

"The day after."

"How long have you known about it?" He took her hand and gently pulled her toward the kitchen. "Never mind. You know, Andy—" He'd given this lecture about fifty times this school year already and it never sunk in. He must be doing something wrong, but he couldn't figure out what to change. "Come on, you need to finish and get to bed."

Her shoulders slumped as she plopped down at the kitchen table and opened her math book. He rubbed the back of his neck. If this was just the beginning of adolescence, he was in for trouble. He'd had custody of Andy since his divorce when she was a baby. They'd always been close, but lately they seemed to regularly be at odds. He wandered into the living room and picked up a purple ceramic dinosaur Andy had made him for Father's Day in the third grade.

"How's that new squash girl?" Andy called.

"Squash girl?"

"That one you knew when you were young."

"You mean Pumpkin?"

"Yeah, her. What's she like?"

"Do your homework."

"I am!" Andy yelled. "So what's she like?"

Mike put the dinosaur down and went into the kitchen. He thought about seeing Pumpkin in the wedding shop and at the heirs' meeting. About taking her to the emergency room and their conversation there. "She's nice."

"Is she pretty?" Andy twirled her pencil.

Very pretty. "I guess so."

"Can't you tell?"

Andy's face registered disgust and he knew he sounded like a dweeb. His daughter could think that of him when she was sixteen, but he wasn't ready for it when she was just eleven. "Okay, she's pretty."

"*Really* pretty?"

"Yes, really pretty," he said, and Andy's eyes grew round.

"Now do your homework."

Andy grinned.

"Who's really pretty?" His mother came up the basement steps with a laundry basket full of folded clothes.

"Pumpkin, the wedding planner," Andy said in a know-it-all voice.

"You're talking about Delaney McBride?" his mother asked.

"Yeah, Dad thinks she's gorgeous. Like a movie star. And he wants to go out with her."

Mike straightened. "Hey, now wait a—"

"L-O-V-E," Andy spelled aloud.

"Michael, is this true?" His mother set the basket on the table and turned to face him.

"Yes." Andy laughed.

"No," Mike said. "Andy, knock it off."

"Michael, are you planning to go out with her?" His mother smiled.

"No." Except he was supposed to be romancing Pumpkin to make sure she stayed in town long enough to do all the weddings. "I mean, I don't know," he said, backtracking. "We just saw each other yesterday for the first time in years." He scowled at his daughter. "Don't go reading anything into this. If I do go out with Pumpkin while she's here, it'll just be because we're friends."

His mom picked up the laundry basket and headed down the hall. "I told you years ago to keep an eye on that one. I knew she would be a beauty someday."

LATE THE NEXT MORNING, Delaney took a break from wedding planning and headed down Main Street toward Uncle Lou's office a few blocks away. The sun was already warming the day and she felt like a tourist as she peered into the shop windows, one after another. She breathed in the sweet smell of just-made fudge and let out a sigh; the fudge alone was reason enough to stay here for two months.

After another couple of blocks, she reached the old brick bank building that housed Uncle Lou's office and headed up the stairs to the second floor.

She pulled open the door and instantly

noticed the richness of the interior—the dark woods, the cordovan leather club chairs, the thick Turkish carpet. This was the office of a man who clearly enjoyed nice things.

"I'm Delaney McBride," she said to the receptionist. "Lou Waverly is my uncle. I'm just wondering if he has a few minutes."

"Oh, Delaney!" The woman stood and shook Delaney's hand. "I'm Claire Hannoway. Lou thought you might be stopping in one of these days." She glanced at the phone on her desk and pointed at a steady red light. "He's been on a conference call for twenty minutes. I don't think it'll be too much longer. Why don't you have a seat and I'll let him know you're here. Would you like a cup of coffee or a water?"

"Water would be fine, thanks." As soon as Delaney settled into one of the club chairs, a small black poodle raced down the hall toward her. The dog wiggled around at her feet, sniffing and snorting, and she reached down to pet his head. He licked her pants and she shifted her leg away.

Claire returned with a bottle of water. "That's your uncle's dog, Blue. He brings him to the office every day."

Delaney took the water and opened it.

Poodles were supposed to be named Fluffy or Foo-foo. Wasn't the name Blue supposed to be reserved for hounds with soulful eyes?

"So you've taken over the wedding planning," Claire said. "How do you like it?"

"For day three, it's not so bad, I guess. This isn't exactly something you learn in school."

"Ellie was quite well-known for the weddings she put on." Claire returned to her desk.

"So I hear." Delaney felt something odd against her calf and looked down to find the dog humping her leg. With one hand, she pushed him gently away. "I'm just going to do the best I can."

"How about the other heirs? How are they doing with their tasks?" Claire filed some papers in the cabinet behind her desk.

"Well…we've all agreed we're in this together. We succeed as a group." A picture of the Henrys fistfighting flashed through her mind. Yeah, they'd succeed all right—at killing one another.

"That will was all the talk when it first got read, what with those stipulations. It was nice of your aunt to remember the Henrys and Mike and Dan. And you, of course. I think everyone was surprised she left Lou out of the will, but then, maybe she thought he didn't need the money."

He *didn't* need the money.

From the hallway came a deep voice. "But I *am* in the will. If the heirs fail, I get everything, whether I need it or not."

Delaney turned to see her great-uncle, still a bear of a man, coming toward her, grinning. How had she been so afraid of him as a kid? He wasn't a grizzly, he was a teddy. She stood to give him a hug.

"I'm glad you stopped by," Lou said. "What'd you do to your wrist?"

"Just a sprain." Delaney followed him to his office and took a seat opposite him at the glass coffee table. "I'm so sorry about Aunt Ellie. Somehow, I always thought she'd live forever."

"We all did. It was a shock. Three months after she got the diagnosis, she was gone." His pain was palpable.

"I didn't even know she was sick." Delaney felt tears spring to her eyes and she blinked them away.

"She didn't want anyone to know. Called it an *inconvenience* that wasn't worth bothering people with. Said there were far more interesting things to be concerned about than an old woman's health."

"That sounds like her."

Silence settled over them for a moment. Then Lou said, "So how's the wedding planning? Everything going all right?"

"Wedding planning is going fine. It's the rest of the will that I'm worried about. That's why I'm here—to ask your advice." She held up her braced wrist and began to describe last night's meeting.

It took only a few minutes for her uncle to confirm what she suspected. Stonewall was a worrier; he fretted even when things were going well. Sully, on the other hand, was an optimist.

"And Henry Clark was a pragmatist," her uncle said. "He'd sit down with the two of them over a bottle of Jameson and pretty soon they'd all be in agreement. Finest Irish whiskey there is, he used to say." Lou smiled. "Not sure whether that'll be much help to you."

She laughed. "I'm not sure, either. But I'll pick up a bottle and keep it on hand in case I get desperate."

"You get desperate about anything and you let me know. I'll do whatever I can to help," he said. "I want all of you to succeed because that's what Ellie wanted."

Delaney cocked her head. "What *did* she

want? I'm still trying to figure out why she wrote a will like this."

"Just eccentric, I guess. You know how some elderly people get."

"She never told you why?"

"I think it was just her way of making one last connection with the people she loved."

She was tempted to say that a conventional will without contingencies would have been an even nicer connection, but she kept her mouth shut.

By the time Delaney headed back to Storybook Weddings fifteen minutes later, she was more determined than ever to fulfill her aunt's wishes. If Jameson was what it took to keep the Henrys in line, she'd buy a bottle a week. Striding down the sidewalk, she passed Hobart & Hobart Garage and Service Station and spotted Dan talking to a customer at the gas pump.

He waved her over. "How's the wrist?"

"Better."

"You want to see your aunt's old Chevy?"

"Sure."

"It's in the fourth bay." He pointed into the garage at a red car with white tail fins and yelled, "Hey, Mike, someone to see you!"

She turned to stare at Dan.

"Just go on in. Mike'll show it to you."

"Thanks." Loads. *Just great.* He'd probably think she was chasing him. "Don't you put those things up in the air?" she asked Dan, stalling.

"We don't have a lift in the fourth bay." He returned to his customer.

Delaney stepped carefully across the stained concrete floor, reaching the Chevy just as Mike rolled out from underneath, flat on his back on a creeper.

He grinned up at her. "Hey, there." He rolled to his feet and pulled a rag from the back pocket of his jeans to wipe off his hands. Then he absently brushed off the seat of his pants. "How's your wrist this morning?"

"Better."

"Good, I'd hate to see you struggling with the weddings because I insisted you come to a meeting. What can I do for you?"

She took in his messy dark hair and his blue eyes and his open smile and his well-worn jeans slung low on his hips and his shirt coming untucked and then she reminded herself of what good friends they were becoming. *No.* "No. I was just passing by. Went to see if my uncle had any advice about the Henrys. And then I saw Dan out in front and he waved me over and asked if I wanted to see the car and so here I am." Why did the truth suddenly sound so much like a lie? She eyed the Chevy so she could avoid looking at him. "Shouldn't you be filing legal briefs or something?"

"That's on the docket for this afternoon. Dan and I wanted to check out a few things on the car, so I came in here first. Did your uncle have any brilliant ideas?"

"Jameson."

"Whiskey?"

She nodded. "Finest Irish whiskey there is."

"Well, if it works, count me in. Maybe I should pick up a bottle before the next heirs' meeting. If it doesn't get the Henrys together, then at least the rest of us can drown our sorrows."

Delaney laughed and turned back to the Chevy. "So this is Uncle Henry's car. I hardly remember him driving it."

"That's because it was already twenty years old when you were born. Your aunt said he kept it because it was the car he courted her in."

Another hopeless romantic. "Will it be hard to fix?"

"For hardly being driven in the past

fifteen years, it's not bad. Needs brakes. Some bodywork. Mice nested in the backseat, so we've got to pull the seat out for reupholstering. The tires are rotted. About what you'd expect."

"About what *you'd* expect. I, on the other hand, would have no clue. Here's what I know about cars—they're red or blue or gold or black—"

"I'd be happy to teach you."

"How to fix cars?

"It's fun. You might like it."

She laughed. "I don't think so. I have enough to learn right now about wedding planning. And if I don't get back to the shop pretty soon, I'm going to fail at that." Mike was wrong. Fixing cars with him wouldn't be fun, it'd be torture. She'd have to see him pull a rag out of his back pocket and not let herself notice how well his jeans fit. She'd have to watch him tighten lug nuts on a wheel and not let herself notice the muscles in his arms. She'd have to listen to what he was teaching her and not let herself notice what a really nice guy he was.

Because if she let herself notice, then she would want him. And that was just plain stupid. She didn't need to tangle up her life like that. Didn't need to experience one more short-term relationship destined to go nowhere.

Should she learn to fix cars with Mike Connery? Not on her life.

CHAPTER FOUR

DELANEY SCOWLED AT the bolts of white and silver netting on the worktable in the back room of Storybook Weddings and had the sudden urge to bite her nails even though she'd broken herself of the habit years ago. She had to cut three hundred five-inch squares out of this netting. And then she had to put five silver and pearl, chocolate-filled after-dinner mints on each square, fold up the sides and tie a silver ribbon around each one. And on each ribbon she had to hang a tiny silver ring as a symbol of unbroken love.

By the time she finished this project, she suspected those rings would symbolize unbroken insanity. *Hers.* A mere three hundred mint packages before Saturday's wedding. Not to mention the other things she had to get done.

All this with a sprained wrist. Thank goodness Megan would be able to help out tomorrow. But once Megan had the baby, Delaney wasn't sure who she would be able to call on. Her stomach churned and she tamped down her panic. Sometimes it was better not to think of things until absolutely necessary.

With a sigh, she picked up the scissors and began to cut out squares. Silver, white, silver, white, silver… "Someone please shoot me now," she muttered. "Six feet under would be preferable to slow death by boredom." Silver, white…

A scraping noise drew her attention and she raised her head to see a young girl in shorts and a T-shirt watching her from the doorway, a backpack slung over one shoulder, her long hair straggling loose from its ponytail. The girl rubbed a sneakered foot against the floor.

"Hi. I didn't know anyone was here," Delaney said. Wasn't that front bell supposed to jangle whenever the door opened? "Can I help you with something?"

The girl shrugged. "What did you mean, that thing about six feet under?"

Delaney blushed. "That…that was about six feet of netting I have to put under the…wedding cake for decoration," she lied. "I talk to myself all the time. I didn't hear you come in. The bell didn't jingle."

"I opened the door really carefully so it wouldn't."

"And why is that?"

"I just wanted to see what you looked like."

"Oh. I'm Delaney McBride. Do I look okay?"

The girl nodded. "I already know who you are. I'm Andrea Connery, but everyone calls me Andy."

Delaney eyed Andy thoughtfully. "Are you related to Mike?"

"He's my dad."

Delaney held in a gasp. Mike had a child? Did he have a wife, too? "Mike's your dad?" She kept her voice casual. "We go back a long time. I've known him since I was five."

"He said you were pretty."

Delaney's cheeks warmed. So did her heart. "That was nice of him."

Andy studied herself in the mirror on a nearby wall. "I hope I'm pretty some day."

"You're pretty now."

Andy snorted. "I know what I look like. And I don't look like the popular girls."

Delaney felt a wave of recognition. This girl was not a blue-eyed blonde, lithe and physically mature beyond her years. "No, you don't. But you know what? Neither did I. And I guess I turned out okay, huh? I mean, your dad said I'm pretty." She continued cutting.

"What are you making?"

"Favors for the wedding guests to take home."

"Or eat."

"Or eat. I need to make three hundred of these things," Delaney said.

Andy let her backpack slide off her shoulder to the floor. "My dad told me you hurt your wrist. I could help you."

Delaney lifted her head, about to decline the offer, but the sight of Mike's blue eyes in the child's face changed her mind. "How old are you?"

"Eleven. I used to help your aunt sometimes. She would have me do stuff for the weddings."

Delaney handed her the scissors. "Well, then, I guess you could help me, too."

Andy pursed her lips. "She paid me five dollars an hour."

Ah. A shrewd businesswoman. She would like this kid whether Mike was her father or not. "Of course. That's only fair."

"She called me when she needed help. Or I would stop by after school and see." Andy bent over the netting and got busy.

"Then, that's what we'll do, too," Delaney said.

The two worked in silence for several minutes. Then Andy asked, "Were you surprised to be in the will?"

"Uh, yeah," Delaney said, taken aback. "I live on the East Coast, so I've only seen my great-aunt a few times since we moved out of town. The will was a shock." *Shock* was an understatement.

"It was around here, too."

Oh, great, the town was talking again. At least the gossip didn't involve her sending love notes to Mike Connery this time.

"Everyone thought she'd leave her money to her brother."

"She probably figured he had enough of his own."

"Maybe." Andy stopped to count her netting squares. "But Claire, his girlfriend—"

"Claire's his girlfriend?"

"Uh-huh. My friend Emma says her mom calls it a *working relationship*. Anyway, Emma's mom said Claire said the money should have stayed in Ellie's family, or something like that."

"I *am* in the family," Delaney said. "Ellie was my great-aunt."

Andy cocked her head. "I bet Claire forgot about that."

An hour later, she and Andy had made real progress, both with the favors and with the latest gossip around town. In the midst of pattering about one person or another, Andy offered up that she'd been born in Chicago and her parents divorced when she was two.

"I'm sorry," Delaney said. "Does your mom live in town?"

"No. She lives in Berlin. She's an international lawyer. I don't see her very often."

Delaney searched for something to say that didn't sound either pitying or cavalier. "That's too bad."

Andy shrugged. "I'm used to it."

Used to not seeing her mother? She didn't doubt that was true, but she suspected there was some bravado talking here, too.

"My other grandma lives in Ohio. I hardly ever see her, either. That's why I like it here." Andy gestured with the scissors. "Because my grandma and grandpa are here. And my auntie Jane comes over all the time because she's only an hour away. She's married and going to have a baby, so then I'll have a cousin."

"Congratulations."

"I hope she still comes to visit as much when the baby is born," Andy said in a low voice.

Delaney raised her head, suddenly realizing the extent of Andy's longing for a mother. "Oh, I'm sure she will."

"Auntie Jane says I have my finger on the pulse of Holiday Bay."

Auntie Jane was right about that. Delaney dropped some mints on the netting square, pulled the four corners to center, slid a silver ring on the ribbon and tied a bow around the little package.

"What does that mean?" Andy looked at her innocently.

Delaney swallowed a laugh. "It means you know what's going on."

"Oh. That's what my grandma says, too."

The bell at the front door jangled and Delaney slipped off her stool and went out into the shop. Late-afternoon sunlight streamed through the picture windows and sparkled on the tiara display. Mike, smiling and dressed in a dark suit and starched white shirt, moved toward her. Quite the change from the dirty jeans and T-shirt he'd been wearing this morning. "Well, hello. I see you've taken on your attorney persona this afternoon," she said.

"Had to go to court. Hey, I wanted to give you a heads-up. My daughter used to help Ellie out around here. If she happens to stop by—"

"She's here. Helping me make favors."

Mike frowned. "That's what I was afraid of. Any excuse not to do homework. Is she in the back?"

Delaney nodded and headed toward the workroom with Mike right behind her. "Hey, Andy, look who I found in the shop."

At the sight of Mike, the girl's face fell. She set the scissors on a pile of netting squares. "Oh. Dad."

Mike stopped in the doorway. "Andy, what are you doing here?"

"She hired me." Andy slid off her stool.

"What about that energy poster you have to make? And the rest of your homework?"

"I can do it later." Andy tossed her ponytail. "How's she supposed to do all this stuff herself with a wrecked wrist?"

"Andrea…" he said, his tone filled with warning.

The tension between the two was unmistakable and Delaney wondered whether Mike fully realized the impact his ex-wife's absence was having on Andy. "She's been a big help, Mike. I'd be way behind if she hadn't stopped by today," she said in a rush. She turned to Andy. "But, honey, your main job has to be school. So if you're going to keep working for me—and I hope you do—you have to finish your homework first. Okay?"

Andy stared at her as if she was a traitor.

"Deal?" Delaney held her breath. "I'm going to need your help around here to get everything done."

Andy huffed and bent to pick up her backpack. "Okay."

"Okay," Delaney said. "See you tomorrow."

When Andy was out the door, Mike shook his head. "Something's going wrong and I can't figure out what it is. One minute she's the same sweet kid she's always been. And the next, she's moody and hates school and me."

"She's a teenager."

"She's *eleven*," Mike said.

"Eleven is the new thirteen."

"If you're right, it's going to be a long road."

Delaney walked with him toward the front door. She didn't want to cause him worry over something he couldn't change, but if she was right about Andy, he should know what he was dealing with. "It might have something to do with her mother being gone."

"She told you about her mother?" He looked stunned.

"Not a lot."

He shook his head. "Not much I can do about it. Her mother took a job in Berlin—international trade attorney for a multinational firm—almost four years ago. What it's become for Andy is an occasional visit or phone call, and presents on her birthday and Christmas."

"I'm sorry."

"It's not your fault. Just the cards we've been dealt." He nodded toward the workroom. "Thanks for what you said back there. That was the least resistance I've seen her put up over homework in the past six months." He opened the door and stepped outside, then stuck his head back in. "You want to go out for a drink sometime?"

A moment passed before she found her voice. "Sure."

"Da-ad! I have homework to do!" Andy yelled from the street.

He rolled his eyes. "I'll talk to you later."

Delaney grinned after him like the village idiot. If she wasn't mistaken, Mike Connery was actually beginning to see her as someone other than Pumpkin McBride, the gnat.

HEAD UNDER THE HOOD of a Taurus in the first bay of Hobart's Garage, Dan glanced at Mike, standing next to the car. "Has Pumpkin said anything about staying to do all five weddings yet?"

"She's only been here two days. Give her some time."

"You need to kick the romance program into gear." Dan reached for the wrench he'd set off to one side, patting his hand around in frustration when it didn't appear under his fingers. "Which, I might add, shouldn't exactly be torturous with the way Pumpkin looks now."

He was right about that. They'd always known Pumpkin was smart, but who would have guessed she'd turn out beautiful? Who, besides his mother, that was. He picked up the wrench and handed it to Dan. "Way ahead of you. I asked her out for a drink."

"Good man." Dan straightened. "Once Pumpkin has the money in hand, she'll probably thank you for getting her to stay."

"Yeah." He felt a twinge of guilt and pushed it away. As long as he kept things between them in control, as long as she never found out that his attentions toward her weren't real, everything would be fine.

EARLY WEDNESDAY AFTERNOON, Delaney sat across the table from this weekend's bride and her mother. The young twentysomething was in a panic over her coming nuptials. A groundless panic, Delaney thought. Because as far as this girl and the mother knew, everything was in place for the perfect event; she had no inkling that her wedding soloist had canceled this morning because of severe laryngitis. Nor did she know that every other singer Delaney had called was already booked for Saturday. No, this bride was creating drama simply because that was what she did. Because she was from a moderately well-to-do family, a spoiled princess with streaked golden hair.

"Mother, it's my *wedding*. I'm only getting married once and I want everything to be perfect," the bride said. She laid an accusing look on Delaney. "No one told us that Mrs. Clark passed on and you were taking over."

The mother patted her daughter's hand. "Honey, I'm sure Miss McBride knows what she's doing."

"Absolutely." Delaney wished she were at the end of this meeting instead of the beginning. "My aunt was very thorough. There's not much I need to do." Well, okay, there was plenty she needed to do, but why distress the bride any further? "In fact, my aunt was so well organized, I should probably stay out of the way and let things run themselves!" She gave them her best I'm-on-your-side smile.

Neither woman smiled back.

"Of course, I mean that only in the rhetorical sense."

"Is the white carriage ready?" The bride began to gnaw at the cuticle on her index finger, then jerked her hand away as if suddenly realizing her nails would be less than perfect on her wedding day. "The tiny bags of pearl and silver mints? The tiered cake with seashells and starfish cascading down the side? And the DJ? Does he know he's supposed to play 'Under the Sea' when we arrive?"

The DJ! A trickle of sweat ran down the center of Delaney's back. She hadn't put a call in to him yet. She forced her lips to stay curved in a smile and dug deep into her limited wedding vocabulary. "Everything is set. Saturday will be a lovely beginning to your life of wedded bliss. There's just…one small detail that came up this morning. Your soprano soloist called and it seems she has laryngitis."

"I knew it!" The bride's voice quavered. "I knew that my perfect wedding—"

"Does that mean she can't sing at all?" the mother asked.

Delaney blinked. *She can croak.* "She can hardly talk. You know, I'd like to think of this as an opportunity to make the wedding even more perfect."

The bride gaped at her and Delaney kept talking. "I know several other excellent singers, so this will be a nonissue in no time. Now—" she stood "—the favors are finished. Let me show them to you."

By the time she got the two women out of the store, Delaney felt like she'd just finished a marathon. It had taken everything she had to keep the bride calm. Now all she had to do was confirm with the DJ and deliver a singer.

Nothing to it.

She couldn't wait to have this first wedding over with.

And the second and the third and the fourth…

Frankly, she wished she could chuck it all and go back to her life in advertising where she felt competent, together and in control. Too bad she had no life in advertising to go back to.

In desperation, she dialed the DJ scheduled for Saturday, The Incomparable Bobby C. Maybe he could help.

By the time he answered on the seventh ring, she was ready to jump through the phone. "I'm so glad you're there! I'm handling the weddings for my late aunt, who owned Storybook Weddings, and I'm just following up to make sure you're—"

"Doing the wedding this weekend?" he asked. "All set. Ocean theme. Beach songs. Let's see… 'Under the Sea' when the couple arrives. The bridal dance is 'Hawaiian Wedding Song.' The parents' dance is 'Beyond the Sea.' Make sure I play the Beach Boys, some reggae and lots of fun dance music."

Delaney let out a sigh. "Thank you! It's such a relief to know I don't have to worry about the reception music."

He laughed. "No. You shouldn't have to worry about any of the suppliers. Ellie Clark was like a general—we were her troops. She was such a perfectionist about her weddings, nobody ever got out of line because they knew she'd replace them in a heartbeat. I'm going to miss her."

"I think a lot of people will," Delaney said. "I could sure use one of her replacements right now." She explained the problem with the soloist. "If you have any thoughts, I'm all ears."

Silence. "Bobby C?" she prodded.

"Yeah. Jeez, I don't know. I could spin a CD if you want. No flat notes guaranteed."

"Thanks, but I don't think that will cut it." Delaney slumped against the wooden desk chair and closed her eyes. Would the bride give her low ratings on the wedding-evaluation form just because the soloist got laryngitis?

For the second time in half an hour, she longed for her old job at the ad agency and her nice, neat desk with the ergonomic chair that hugged and supported her as she worked.

"Hey, Delaney, do you need me to work today?"

She jerked upright and looked directly at Andy, just two feet away. "Jeez, Andy, you're going to give me a heart attack. How do you get in that door without making the bell ring?"

Andy laughed as though proud of herself. She dropped her backpack on the floor.

Delaney shook her head. "Homework before anything else."

"Awww—"

"Get your books out. I'm not getting in trouble with your dad." She watched as Andy unzipped her backpack. "You don't happen to know any singers, do you?" she asked in desperation. "The soloist for Saturday's wedding has laryngitis."

Andy scrunched up her face. "You could ask my dad. He was in the band."

"He played trumpet, honey. He wasn't a singer."

"He can sing, too."

"We all can—in the shower." Delaney shook her head.

"He's pretty smart. Maybe he'll have an idea."

"Unless he's got a singer tucked away somewhere, all the good ideas in the world aren't going to help me."

Andy shrugged. "What else are you going to do?"

Leave it to a kid to cut to the chase. "Well, I…" What *was* she going to do? "When does your dad get home from work?"

"Wednesdays he plays baseball for Ollie's Tap. Afterward he goes to the bar and my grandma stays with me. You could go to the game tonight."

Mike was still playing baseball? Back in high school, she used to sit in the bleachers and fantasize that when he waved at the fans in the stands, he was waving at her. Watching him play had been the high point of her summer nights. It would be fun to see him on the field again. Besides, he had asked her about going for a drink. "I suppose it wouldn't hurt if I talked to your dad about a singer. Who knows what he might come up with?" She gave a cavalier toss of her head. "So…what time is the game?"

DELANEY SAT IN HER BMW in Ollie's parking lot but made no move to go into the bar. A breeze slipped through the open windows, soft, like cotton sheets on naked skin when the heat of the day has lingered well beyond darkness. It was the kind of night for falling in love.

She thought of Drew, the man she'd dated for two years—until he'd decided that what he wanted to be was friends with benefits. And before him, Will, who got so settled in their relationship it ceased being a relationship. And before him, Christopher, who broke up with her and married some woman he'd only known for three weeks. And a host of other dates that only served to reinforce what she'd learned at her mother's knee: there was only one person you could rely on in this world. Yourself.

She closed her eyes a moment. But sometimes, on nights like this when the sky was full of stars and summer was in the air and everything seemed flush with promise, she wished she had gotten it all wrong, that love could start and not end, that there really was such a thing as a happy ending.

And then, she would be smart enough to put that thought completely out of her mind.

A couple of players wearing Ollie's pinstriped jerseys crossed the lot, obviously in high spirits. They must have won their game. As the men pulled open the door to the bar, music from the jukebox escaped out into the night, then was quickly recaptured as the door swung shut.

She hadn't gone to the game after all. Had spent so long vacillating about whether or not to go that all she had time to do was show up at the bar afterward. So here she was.

In the parking lot.

She peered up at the tavern sign shining in the darkness, at the blinking neon signs illuminating the windows. Mike was in there, her first infatuation. She almost wished he hadn't asked her to go for a drink the other day because she didn't want him to think she was using the soloist problem as an excuse to chase him down in the bar. After all, she could have just as easily asked for his help by phone.

Well, if he read anything into her coming here tonight, that was *his* problem. Because she wasn't infatuated with him anymore. No way. And as soon as these weddings were through, she would be headed back to Boston, chasing down the future she'd put on hold to come here.

She shoved open her car door and stepped out.

MIKE TOASTED THE TEAM'S win with Dan, then leaned his elbows on the bar and took a big swallow of his Spotted Cow beer. "I'm still trying to figure out why Ellie wrote this will. If she wanted us to have the car, why didn't she just give it to us?"

"Maybe she wanted to make sure we'd bring it back to its former glory," Dan said over the music.

"She had to realize we would have fixed it up no matter what."

Dan shrugged. "Well, none of it makes sense. Look at the Henrys. The only thing they get when all is said and done is the satisfaction that the city has a new band shell."

"They do get the chance to work together." Mike grinned.

Dan finished off his beer and pushed the glass toward the bartender for a refill. "Yeah, that's going to be pleasant for everyone involved."

"Hey, check it out," Mike said, and nodded at a table in the dining area across the bar. Sully and his wife were having burgers with Pumpkin's great-uncle Lou. Mike waved. "All we need is Stonewall and Pumpkin and we could hold an heirs' meeting."

"What do you think Ellie was trying to do with Pumpy? Having to come here for two months is a burden when you have a job," Dan said.

"Maybe Ellie wanted to force her to make a tough decision."

Dan played with the coaster on the bar. "What?"

"Her job versus her inheritance. Her high-powered life versus the excitement of Holiday Bay. I don't know. I'm just talking. I have no idea." Mike took another swallow of his beer.

"So how many days until you start setting the hook?" Dan swiveled on his bar stool and surveyed the crowd bar.

Mike frowned. "What hook?"

"Pumpkin. When are you having that drink?"

"Oh, yeah. She's too busy until this wedding is over."

"Don't wait too long. We can't risk her throwing in the towel." Dan glanced at the front door, then slid off his bar stool. "There's Megan."

Mike watched as Dan sneaked up behind his wife and planted a kiss on the back of her neck. She started, then twisted round to kiss him full on the mouth.

He felt a sudden wistfulness and turned away, his thoughts on the woman he once loved, the woman his love couldn't keep. Cassie had already been pregnant with Andy when they married and he'd foolishly thought that once the baby was born they'd become a family, tied to one another by love. Before two years were out, Cassie left him and Andy, determined to make her way to the top of the legal profession.

Dan leaned in next to him. "Don't look now, but you've just been handed the opportunity of a lifetime. Check out the door."

Mike shifted his gaze. Pumpkin stood inside the door looking more than a little lost.

"Seems to me like she needs a friend."

Without another word or a sideways glance, Mike got up and began to work his way toward her through the crowd.

CHAPTER FIVE

"CAN I GET YOU A DRINK?"

Delaney turned toward the voice at her left. Mike. In his short-sleeved jersey, it was obvious he still had the physique of an athlete. Her heart skipped a beat. Oh, brother, her reactions to him were like muscle memory. "Uh, sure. How about a Diet Coke?"

He raised his brows. "We won tonight. And you're having a Diet Coke?" He grinned and his blue eyes began to make her melt, just as they had when she was a kid. Old habits certainly died hard. "When in Rome…" he said.

God, he was cute. She laughed. "All right. Make it a rum and Diet Coke." Her mind might need a little numbing before this night was over.

"Better. Come on." He led her to where Megan and Dan were sitting at the bar. "Anyone want anything?"

"I'll take another water," Megan said.

Dan held up his nearly full beer bottle and shook his head.

Mike moved to an empty spot at the bar and waved at the bartender.

"How's the wedding planning coming along?" Dan asked Delaney over the din.

She frowned. "Not so good at the moment. The soloist canceled—she's got laryngitis."

Megan gasped. "But I was there today. When did this happen?"

"About an hour after you left. I would have called, but I knew you were at a doctor's appointment." She shook her head. "I called every singer on my aunt's list. They're all booked. I've got just one day to fix this before our inheritances collapse like a reception tent in a tornado."

"This might not mean the end," Megan said. "The whole thing is about love and commitment, not about who sings the songs."

"Yes, well, I'm not sure this bride and you are of the same opinion," Delaney said. "For her, it's more about the soloist and the flowers. And the white carriage and the seashells on her cake. And woe to the wedding planner who doesn't deliver."

"Doesn't deliver what?" Mike handed her a tumbler.

"Doesn't deliver the fairy-tale wedding she's expecting." Delaney used the skinny red straw to stab at the lime wedge floating in her drink.

Mike looked from Delaney to Megan to Dan. "Am I missing something?"

Delaney took a sip of her drink and savored the taste. Then she took another, larger sip. "Here's the thing," she said. "It's the soloist." She proceeded to fill Mike in. "So my question is. Actually it's *questions*. First, do you know where I can get a soloist on short notice? And second, if we end up without a singer at the wedding and the bride gives me a zero in the music category on the evaluation form, will it lower my score enough to mean the gig is up?"

Mike drank his beer, a perplexed expression on his face.

"Let's think about this," Dan said. "If a wedding takes place in the woods and there isn't anyone to hear the music, is there really a wedding?"

"Drink your beer and shut up," Mike said. "I don't suppose a bad score in one category would doom you. But what if the bride gets so upset about the missing soloist that she marks you down in several categories?"

"As long as the vows are said, I'd call it a

successful wedding." Dan put his arm around his wife. "Wouldn't you, hon?"

"Yes. But it's not what we think that matters," Megan said.

"Right. And like I said before, this particular bride might disagree with you." Delaney couldn't keep the discouragement out of her voice.

"I guess that's why your aunt made up that form. To make the process less subjective," Mike said.

"Except for on the part of the bride," Megan pointed out.

"This endless speculation isn't helping me find a soloist. Don't you guys know anyone who can sing? At this point I'm not asking for a fantastic voice, just one good enough to carry a tune. I can always tell the pianist to play louder to hide any flat notes." She turned to Megan.

"Don't look at me!" Megan said. "If I sing, I'll empty the church. But, Mike, how about—"

"No."

"No, who?" Delaney asked.

"Why not?" Megan grinned.

"Who? And why not?" Delaney pressed. "Come on, Mike, I'm at my wit's end here. All choices must be brought forward and I will eliminate them once I know what they are."

"She's right," Dan said. "Might be the only shot we have."

"Who?" Delaney raised her eyebrows.

Mike grimaced. "Me."

"You…? Andy implied the same thing. You mean you truly can sing?"

"Like a nightingale," Megan said.

"Only lower," Dan added.

Delaney stared at them. "This is a joke, right?"

Dan and Megan shook their heads.

"When did this happen?" Delaney asked, incredulous.

Mike shrugged. "I started growing into it my senior year."

"By college, he could've been in a boy band." Dan did an upper-body dance move.

Mike snorted.

Delaney felt a flicker of hope. She looked at Megan. "Does he sing well enough to do a wedding?"

"The boy could have a nice side business if he wanted one."

"Okay, then," Delaney said to Mike. "You're hired. I'll get you the songs. You'll have two days to practice."

"Wait a minute."

"You have a better idea?"

He opened his mouth and closed it without saying a word, then took a gulp of beer.

"That's what I thought. Don't worry. There's only four songs."

"Four? When am I going to learn them?"

"Relax. They're all standard wedding fare. You probably already know every one. I'll drop off the sheet music in the morning." Delaney swallowed more of her drink. "You can read music, can't you?"

"Well enough."

"It doesn't have to be so much, anyway. Old Mrs. Keely, the pianist, said she'd practice with whoever I found to sing." She smiled brightly at Mike so he wouldn't have the heart to change his mind.

"I think it only appropriate that we celebrate Mike's foray into his new singing career with another drink," Dan said. He raised a hand for the bartender and ordered just as Sully and Delaney's uncle Lou approached.

"You kids seem awfully serious for having just won a ball game," Sully said to Mike. He turned to Delaney. "How's your wrist?"

"I don't have time to think about it," she said.

"I'm already onto new problems. The soloist for Saturday's wedding canceled—laryngitis."

Lou's mouth dropped open. "What'll you do?"

"Mike's going to sing."

"Mike?" Sully put a hand on Mike's shoulder. "Didn't know you had it in you."

"Well, it remains to be seen," Mike said wryly.

"He's the best I've got," Delaney said.

The bartender returned with two beers, a rum and Diet Coke and a water. "You gentlemen want something?" Dan asked.

"No, thanks," Sully said. "We've still got dinner to finish. Just thought we'd say hi."

Two hours later, Delaney was still at the tavern, sipping her fourth rum and Diet Coke and thinking she was glad her apartment was walking distance away. She'd pick up her car in the morning. She leaned against a support pillar and watched Mike and Dan finish a wobbly game of pool.

"Six ball in the side pocket." She pointed with her drink. The ad agency where she'd worked had a pool table in the lounge; they had a TV, too, but on breaks, everyone played pool.

Mike bent over the table, index finger of his left hand crooked over the stick to guide his shot. He squinted up at her. "You know how to play?"

"A little. Up for another game?"

He dropped the ball in the pocket. After a few more shots, he put the game away, then sidled over to Delaney. "Think you can play with that wrist of yours?"

She saw the challenge in his eyes and met it with her own. "Rack 'em. What's the forfeit?"

He looked at her in surprise, then became thoughtful, as though considering a number of options.

"How about a kiss?" Megan said.

Delaney, Dan and Mike all turned to her at once.

Delaney shook her head. "Oh, no."

"Now that's a novel bet. I like it. Mike?" Dan's expression was all mischief.

Mike's gaze met Delaney's. In the darkness of the bar, his eyes were no longer blue. They were black—dangerous black. He nodded slowly. "Yeah, okay, a kiss. *When* I win you have to kiss me."

She rolled her eyes. Kissing Mike was out of the question. Her knees would probably give out from under her and she'd end up on the floor, the same blithering, infatuated teenager she'd once been. But she'd avoid the problem by winning. Shouldn't be a problem—she'd had some great teachers at the agency. "Okay. You're on."

Dan waved his beer bottle at them both. "And if Delaney wins, Mike has to kiss her."

She tightened her grip on her glass. "No, no, no. Each person names their own forfeit. If I win, you…you…" She racked her brain for something appropriate.

"Have to wash and wax Delaney's BMW," Megan said. She tossed a wicked grin Delaney's way, then placed her attention squarely on Mike. "Shirtless. Barefoot. And in running shorts, those short navy-blue ones with the rip up the right leg." She leaned over to whisper in Delaney's ear, "Have you ever seen him without a shirt on?" She fanned herself.

Just using her imagination made Delaney faint enough. The real thing would probably do her in.

"Okay, then, we have an agreement. A kiss on the lips for a car wash almost in the buff," Dan said. "Rack 'em up."

"You break," Mike said.

Heart pounding, she set her drink on a nearby table, chose a cue stick and chalked the end.

"Need any tips?" Mike took a swallow of his beer.

"I think I'll be okay." She rested the cue across the brace on her wrist and took aim, concentrating hard to clear the rum from her head, if that was even possible. Then she made the opening break, neatly pocketing the nine and leaving the cue ball centered on the table—in perfect position to make a couple more shots.

Mike looked at her, impressed. "Somehow," he said, "I'm thinking you've played more than a little."

"Somehow, I think you're right." She sent another two balls into pockets. Dan let out a whoop. "Mikey, you may have just met your match."

She missed her next shot and glared at Dan. "Your turn, Mike."

He stepped around the table, studying his options. Delaney watched his hands as he chalked his cue—strong hands. She wondered what it would feel like to have one of those hands wrapped around one of hers. To have both of those hands touching her.

Mike deftly sent the three ball into the corner pocket and she jerked her attention back to the game. He dropped another ball in before missing the next shot. A couple of guys from the neighboring pool table stopped playing to watch the game. Within minutes, word of their bet had spread throughout the bar and a large audience had gathered.

She raised her chin and gestured with her stick. "Ten ball in the side pocket," she said with smug confidence.

He smiled as though he knew better. She lined up to shoot and promptly missed. A groan went up among the spectators. Damn, he *did* know better.

Mike gave her a smirk, then began to methodically clear the table. One ball after another dropped into a pocket. For the first time in the game, she began to feel the heat. Working at the agency, she'd gotten pretty good at pool—and she liked to win.

Scratch that. She hated to lose.

At anything.

Now he had only one ball left to play before the eight. Her heart began to pound; this absolutely could not be happening. She stared at the table, willing him to miss his last shot, yet knowing that, deep inside, she actually hoped he would make it.

He chalked his cue, then bent to the table. The room hushed until the only sound was that of the jukebox playing "Money." Then he drove the final ball into the corner pocket and took aim at the eight.

Miss, miss, miss, she willed the ball.

As if taunting her, the round black traitor dropped into the pocket.

A cheer went up from the watching crowd and Dan clapped Mike on the back. Mike grinned at her from across the pool table, then sauntered around to her side to collect his due. He looked down at her, a self-satisfied smirk on his lips. "I believe you owe me something."

She grimaced.

"You're not going to try to get out of it, are you?" he asked.

"I always pay my debts," she said in low voice.

The audience hooted and a smattering of clapping followed. Delaney rose on tiptoe, put her hands on Mike's shoulders and pressed a chaste kiss to his mouth. The warm feel of his lips stunned her, and the thought raced through her mind that she should just kiss him, really kiss him the way she wanted to, audience be damned.

Right, and make an even bigger fool of yourself now than you did as a teenager.

She began to pull away, but Mike's hands closed around her waist and pulled her up against him. His body was lean and hard, and the intimacy of the contact made her breath come faster.

"*That* was not a kiss," he said.

The fan club tittered.

"Yes, it was," she protested.

"Not a forfeit kiss."

He dipped his head toward hers. "This is a forfeit kiss," he said. "Pay attention."

She held herself stiffly, terrified she might make a spectacle of herself in front of all these people.

As he covered her mouth with his, every coherent thought in her head evaporated. His lips slid over hers, gently at first, then insistently pushing her to respond. With the smallest of sighs, she let herself relax, let her hands slide up the muscles of his arms and over his shoulders. He pressed her tightly to him and his tongue teased her lips, played with her mouth until she opened to him. Then he kissed her soundly, dragging her with him into a dark, dizzying place. And then, at the very moment she would have agreed to anything he might have proposed, he let go of her and grinned.

"*That,* Pumpy, was a forfeit kiss," he said, and picked up his beer.

She took a step back and tried to pull herself

together, tried to drag her rum-sodden brain back to coherency so she could snap out a clever comeback. But her usually well-ordered thoughts were jumbled beyond rescue.

"Forfeit kiss?" Megan said loudly. "I think she just paid in advance for her next ten losses!" The throng roared, then dissipated, everyone going back to what they'd been doing before—drinking, chatting, darts and more drinking.

"Well, that was quite something." Megan giggled.

Quite something indeed, Delaney thought. She'd been a spectacle once again. How could she still react to Mike after fifteen years? Other people got over their childhood crushes. Why not her?

She looked for Mike and found him already locked in conversation with Sully, as though a very public passionate kiss was just business as usual for him and, step up, ladies, who's next?

As though reading her thoughts, Megan nodded toward Mike. "You know, he hasn't had a serious relationship since his divorce eight years ago."

"None?"

"Well, he's dated a couple of women. But nothing serious."

No wonder everyone in the bar had been

so into the bet. But what did it matter anyway? This wasn't her town, these weren't her friends. This was Mike's town, his friends. And tonight that had become as clear as the crystal stemware with the bride and groom's names etched into them. She made a show of checking her watch. "I'm going to take off. Too much to do tomorrow."

"I'm right behind you." Megan yawned. "I can't stay up this late anymore." She went to find Dan.

Delaney glanced one more time in Mike's direction, then headed out the door. She couldn't be like this. Couldn't keep thinking wishfully about Mike.

Outside, the clear night sky still glittered with stars and Delaney looked up to search for Orion's belt, then his arms and legs and the bow he carried. The belt was always easy to find, but spotting the rest took a lot more effort. God, but the sky was gorgeous tonight. An astronomer's sky. *A lovers' sky.*

She lowered her gaze and cut through the parking lot past her car, forcing her gait to remain steady. No reason to drive, not with her head full of rum and home only a few blocks away.

All she'd wanted when she came to

Holiday Bay was to finish the weddings and get her inheritance. And then Mike had to step in and complicate everything with a kiss.

Oh, for God's sake, the kiss meant nothing at all. She knew that. The guy still called her Pumpy. That alone should be enough to show her how he truly felt about her.

MIKE PAUSED IN HIS conversation with Sully and looked around for Pumpkin. He hadn't been talking that long; where had she gone?

Megan leaned close and spoke loudly so he could hear her over the music. "She left."

He was shocked at the disappointment he felt. That made twice in fifteen minutes he'd been surprised at his response to something Pumpkin had done.

The first time had been when she kissed him. The feel of her mouth on his, that first little kiss, had only made him want to knock down her walls. So he'd deepened the kiss. And what he'd gotten was a response so un-inhibited he'd taken it to another level…

"She's probably still in the parking lot." Sully rubbed a hand over his abundant chins and raised his eyebrows.

Dan leaned into the conversation. "Keep up the good work. I knew you had it in you."

"What are you waiting for?" Sully asked.

Mike shrugged and hurried outside, crunched across the gravel lot, searching. Hell. Pumpkin's car was still there, but she wasn't in it. She must have decided to walk home. He hoped she hadn't gone away mad. Tomorrow he'd stop by the shop, make up some excuse about the will and try to gauge her frame of mind.

EARLY THE NEXT MORNING, Delaney pulled open the door to the waiting room of Hobart & Hobart's. Sounded like a law firm. Fortunately, there was no way anyone would ever mistake this place for a legal office. She'd just come from Mike's immaculate office with its cherry furniture, glass-tabled waiting room and pleated shades, and the difference between the two establishments couldn't have been more extreme. She stepped across the grimy floor, past the row of molded-plastic chairs along the windows and the table in the corner stacked with old faded magazines and a dingy coffeemaker. Not much had changed since Dan's dad had owned the place. Probably the same coffeemaker. Probably even the same magazines.

Mike's secretary had said he wouldn't be

in until after one, that he had something to do on the Chevy this morning. Much as Delaney had been tempted to leave the sheet music for Saturday's wedding at his office so she wouldn't have to face him, she knew the sooner he had it, the better for everyone. Even if he had to practice singing from underneath a car, at least he'd be practicing.

Maybe she'd be lucky and Mike wouldn't even be here yet. She cheered at the thought. In the light of day, she was even more embarrassed about last night's kiss. As long as Dan assured her that Mike was truly coming in this morning, she'd just leave the music with Dan.

She reached for the door to the garage and stopped. Maybe she could just call the pianist and have her contact Mike about the music. Yeah, and maybe she should stop being such a chicken and get on with it.

She yanked open the door and spotted Dan in the first bay under the open hood of a silver something. A tan car was in the second bay, a white minivan in the third, and she could see the front end of the red Chevy in the fourth, but, as far as she could tell, nobody else was around.

"Hey, Dan," she said.

He lifted his head and straightened, an air gun in his hand. "Well, if it isn't our resident pool shark. Remind me not to challenge you at poker. What can I do for you?"

She held up the yellow envelope of sheet music. "I've got the music for Mike—for the wedding Saturday. His secretary said he was here. Can I leave it with you?"

He jerked his thumb over his shoulder. "You can give it to him yourself. He's right over there."

"Where?" She squinted across the garage.

"Where else? Under your uncle Henry's car again."

Shoot.

"You want me to yell for him?"

"Never mind." Delaney reluctantly walked past the silver car, the tan car, the white minivan and up to the red Chevy. She bent over the open front end and stared at the engine. Then she moved to the side of the car where she could see Mike's feet sticking out. "Hey, Mike," she said loud enough to be heard over the air gun Dan was using. "I've got that sheet music for the wedding and I'll just leave it on the front—"

Mike shot out from under the car, rolled off the creeper and onto his feet. He grinned, and she wished his grin came with a kiss and a profession of love… *Please stop.*

He tugged a faded red rag from the back pocket of his pants and wiped off his hands. She thrust the envelope at him.

"If you want to run though the music with the pianist, give me a call," she said in a rush. "Anytime after three today or tomorrow morning works for her. If you don't have time, the rehearsal's at six-thirty tomorrow night and it will have to do. I called the bride and she is, believe it or not, okay with you singing. Of course, she does think you do this all the time, so she has somewhat of a false sense of security but—"

"And good morning to you, too," he said.

"Sorry. Morning."

He opened the envelope and flipped through the sheets. "You were right—I know all these songs. A little practice and I'll be ready to go."

"And you actually can sing?" The question sounded harsh spoken out loud and she instantly regretted it.

Thankfully, he laughed. "You want to hear me?"

She clasped her hands together and raised her arms in a circle over her head. "No. I'm happy in my bubble, believing that I've solved this problem. No bubble bursting allowed two days before the wedding."

She slid a hand along the Chevy's gleaming white tail fin. "This is one beautiful car. No wonder you and Dan always wanted it."

"1957 Bel Air convertible. Only forty-seven thousand of these babies were ever made." He took a couple of steps toward the front end. "Has a legendary small-block V-8 engine, generally considered the most famous Chevrolet engine of all time."

She raised her brows. "I'm impressed."

He began to amble around the car, motioning with his hand and speaking as though he were one of those models on a rotating platform at an auto show. "Power steering. Power brakes. At an overall length of two hundred inches, this car is roomy, fuel-efficient and tastefully designed with chrome headliner bands on the hardtop, chrome spears on the front fenders, chrome window moldings and—" he pointed at a wheel "—full chrome wheel covers. Plus—" he leaned into the car, pressed the horn and the sound echoed against the tall ceilings of the garage "—a working horn. List price—$2,238. Can I set you up with one?"

"I'll take two." Delaney laughed.

He studied her for a moment. "You took off quick last night."

She knew her cheeks were turning pink and she willed the blush to stop. "It was kind of late. I got to thinking about everything I needed to do today and decided I'd better get some sleep."

"You weren't upset?"

"About what? It was all harmless fun." No way was she going to let him know the effect his kiss had on her.

"It *was* fun. We should do it again."

She blinked. What? Go to the bar? Play pool? Kiss in front of a large group of spectators?

An awkward silence settled over them. Mike wiped his hands on the rag again. "So you want to cruise the av'? When I get the car drivable?"

Thank goodness, a new topic. "As long as you put the top down. I'll dig out my poodle skirt and bobby socks."

"Okay. We'll go out for a milk shake. Maybe I'll even put the moves on you."

Was Mike Connery flirting with her? Or was he just trying to make up for his actions last night? Did she even want to know?

Yeah, she wanted to know. She wanted to know more than she'd ever wanted to know anything in her life. She looked him square in the eye. "You're on."

CHAPTER SIX

"THANK YOU FOR EVERYTHING!" The bride threw her arms around Delaney. "It was perfect. Everything was perfect! Even the soloist. You were right—he was wonderful."

Delaney hugged her back.

"I'm sorry I've been such a pain," the young woman said. "I was just so nervous!"

"You weren't a pain at all," Delaney said in the cheeriest voice she could muster. What could be more perfect than a white lie on a wedding day?

She watched the bride tug up her strapless dress and prance away to talk to a guest. "Don't forget to rate me generously on the evaluation form," she muttered.

She yawned. A few days ago she thought she'd never survive this huge wedding and now it was almost over. Surely half the town had attended. Dinner for three hundred had been served, the cake—with its exquisite cascade of seashells—had been cut, the garter and bouquet tossed, the wedding dance held, and now the crowd was filtering down as the DJ played his last set. She cast her gaze over the reception hall. All she had left to do was pack up the gifts and she was finished. She'd pulled off the first wedding without a hitch except that minor problem with the soloist.

And as it turned out, that hadn't been a problem at all. Not once Mike took over. She couldn't believe what a nice voice he had. Hidden all those years in high school behind the mouthpiece of a trumpet. Stifling another yawn, Delaney headed down the hall for the janitor's closet to find boxes to pack the gifts in.

Hard to believe her ultraorganized great-aunt hadn't put storage bins on the basic wedding-day checklist. Luckily the facility manager had told her where she could find some.

She opened the door to the closet and pulled the string hanging from the ceiling. A single bare bulb glared in the small dark space. Though the overriding smell was one of soap and bleach, the room was a model of dinginess. Partially closing the door behind her, she stepped inside and looked around in frustration. Not exactly a treasure trove of boxes.

One small carton sat in the corner and she picked it up and tapped it upside down on the floor to dislodge any dust or spiders. She began to rummage through the shelves in search of plastic trash bags, making a mental note to add extra-large garbage bags to her list of necessities. No doubt the list would get longer with every wedding she completed.

She finally spotted the bags behind a big pail of cleaner, threw three into the empty carton and shut off the light. She reached for the door just as she heard a woman in the hall say, "A few more weddings and she's going out of business, anyhow."

Delaney froze, just inside the cracked-open door. *A few more weddings and she's going out of business?* They had to be talking about Storybook Weddings.

Another voice murmured something so low she couldn't make out the words. She held her breath and strained to hear as the voices moved farther away.

"Just be patient," a woman whispered. "If she has any more problems like this one, the handwriting will be…"

Delaney exhaled and gulped in some more

air. She inched closer to the door to hear better. In the darkness, she stared at the tiny shaft of hall light cutting across the janitor's-room floor.

Now, all she could make out were mur-murings.

Was this just a couple of locals gossiping? Or was it something else, someone hoping she would fail? She rolled her eyes. Clearly, she was overtired and had seen way too many movies. In the context of a complete conver-sation, the snippets she'd heard probably meant nothing. Time to get back to work. Although, if she could get a glimpse of who was out there talking, well, that would be okay, too. It might be handy information to know someday.

Just in case.

She tucked the box under her arm, pulled open the door and charged into the hall.

And instantly crashed into someone.

She stumbled back. The box went flying and she threw her hands up in front of her face. Mike.

He grabbed hold of both her arms to keep her from falling. "What are you doing?"

For crying out loud. "Shush." She put a finger to her lips and jerked Mike into the janitor's closet, shoving the door shut behind them.

"Well, now, this is interesting," he whispered into the darkness. "Don't you think we'd be more comfortable at my place?"

"Don't be silly," she said, as much to herself as to him. She groped about in the air until her fingers closed around the string, then gave it a tug. Harsh light flooded the room, temporarily blinding them both.

"I didn't hurt your wrist, did I?" Mike asked.

"No, it's almost healed. But what are you doing here? I thought you were gone."

"I think the more logical question is, what are *you* doing here?"

"Listening."

"To what? Mice?"

"To those two women down the hall. I hope they didn't notice it was me coming out of this room."

"The hall was empty," Mike said. "And even if it wasn't, all anyone would've seen was a blur. I think I should start calling you Flash." He shook his head. "So what were you listening to?"

She recounted the conversation. "Do you think it means anything?"

"No. Just some busybodies gossiping about

how the soloist got sick and I had to take over." He grinned like an excited child. "Did they say anything about how I sounded?"

She snorted. "No. And the more I think about it, the more I think it wasn't just gossiping. Their tone was different. More like..."

"Like...major league baseball wanting me to sing at the World Series?"

She slapped his arm.

"Like...music moguls wanting to give me a recording contract?"

"Stop it. This is serious."

"I *am* serious."

"This was more sinister." She nodded to emphasize her words. "They were talking about a *she*. Maybe it has something to do with me. My childhood."

He let out a laugh. "No one cares about your childhood anymore, Pumpkin."

Clearly he did or he might have moved beyond the Pumpkin nickname by now. "Maybe..." She shook her head. "Maybe it has to do with the inheritance. Because if I don't complete the weddings..."

"All the money goes to Ellie's brother. I'd like to point out he doesn't need the money."

"Yeah. And he did offer to help us."

"Well, that's the end of that conspiracy

theory." Mike pulled open the door. "Come on, let's get out of here."

Delaney followed him into the hall and stopped to pick up the box she'd dropped. "So what are you doing here? It's almost midnight. I thought you went home after dinner."

"Hell, with all your spy antics, you almost made me forget. I came back to show you something." He drew a folded sheet of paper from the inside chest pocket of his windbreaker and handed it to her.

Delaney set the box back on the floor and unfolded the sheet. "The bride's evaluation form? She turned it in already? I didn't think we'd see it for at least a week."

"Apparently they were so pleased with the wedding, the mother filled the form out during the reception, then called the executor. He's out of town, so he called me. He thought we might want to get it—"

"Before they had a chance to review their ratings in the cold light of morning. He was right about that." Delaney skimmed to the bottom where the final score was marked. She'd passed with flying colors!

A smile slipped across her face and she laughed delightedly. She threw her arms around Mike, then danced away. "I feel like I just passed my first-quarter exams."

"Congratulations. And you have a whole week before the next one."

"You know, this wasn't so hard, after all. Thanks for all your help." She touched his arm. "Especially for singing at such short notice."

"Dare I say, I see a touch of enthusiasm for wedding planning from Pumpkin McBride?"

"Ah, no. What you see is a touch of enthusiasm because I'm one step closer to getting my inheritance." And one step closer to getting her finances back in control and her life back where she wanted it.

EARLY MONDAY MORNING, Mike swung into the garage to find Dan and Lou Waverly bent over the engine of the '57 Chevy. Lou's black poodle was bouncing at their feet, wrapping its leash around their ankles. Mike stepped toward them, his leather-soled loafers making hardly a noise on the floor. "Hey, you two, what's up?"

"Just showing Lou the resident classic." Dan unwrapped the leash from his legs.

"Used to have a Bel Air Coupe myself," Lou said. "This sure brings back memories. Mine was all black—black and chrome. What a car. I wasn't smart enough to hang on to it, though. Be worth a pretty penny if I had."

Just like this one would be when it was done. "Yeah, they're hard to find now," Mike said.

The dog tried to jump up on him and he blocked it with a knee. Stupid mutt.

"Looks like you're making real progress on the restoration." Lou moved slowly around the car with Dan at his side.

"Slow but sure," Mike said. "We're getting there."

"Brake liners today. And new tires," Dan said. "We're almost ready for a test drive."

"It's going to be a beaut restored. If you two ever want to sell it, let me know."

Mike exchanged a glance with Dan. "Not a chance. We've wanted this car for too long," he said.

"You boys are lucky. I should have hung on to mine," Lou repeated, running a hand over the hood. "I hear Stonewall and Sully aren't getting along so well."

"They're speaking," Mike said.

Dan coughed. "Shouting, anyway. It's a start."

Lou raised an eyebrow. "You want me to talk to them? I've known those guys a long time."

So much for Pumpkin's conspiracy theory.

Lou wouldn't offer to help if he wanted them to fail. "You can try."

"I'll give them both a call once I get to the office."

"You want a ride back?" Dan asked.

Lou headed through the open overhead door out into the lot, the dog prancing on its leash beside him. "No, thanks. It's a nice day for a walk."

"I'll let you know when the Lexus is ready," Dan called after him.

Mike waited until Lou was well up the street before turning to Dan. He owed it to Pumpkin to at least ask. "How'd you end up showing him the car?"

"He wanted to see it."

"He did?"

Dan lifted a set of keys off the rack on the wall and squinted at Mike as if he'd lost his mind. "Everyone asks about it."

"Right. He ask anything else?"

"No. Like what?"

"I don't know. Pumpkin overheard some women talking and thinks there might be a…" It dawned on him that he was about to sound as ridiculous as Pumpkin had in the janitor's closet.

"A what?"

Mike winced. "A plot…to keep us from meeting the terms of the will."

"A plot. Of course. And the Russians are behind it?"

"Maybe Lou Waverly."

Dan choked out a laugh. "Never in a million years. He doesn't need the money and he'd never do it."

"That's what I told her. So humor me here. He didn't say anything suspicious?"

Dan feigned shock. "Now that you mention it… Right after he said he needed an oil change, he said something like, 'Hey, Dan, I'm trying to deep-six everyone's inheritance, but you have to promise not to tell anyone. Pinky swear—'"

"Okay. I get it."

"Then he laid out the entire plan for me."

"I get it."

"You don't *seriously* think he's working that angle, do you?" Dan popped open the hood on a Toyota Camry and checked the oil.

"No."

"Because if you did, I'd have to *seriously* question your sanity."

A CAR HORN BLARED in front of the wedding shop and Delaney looked up from her to-do list. Didn't people know they weren't supposed to blow their horns unless it was an emergency? She bent over her list again, only to be startled by the sound once more. "Jeez!" This time the horn beat out a rhythm. She pushed her chair back and went to the wide storefront window.

Out in front, Mike was leaning against the driver's door of Uncle Henry's red Chevy convertible. An unlit cigarette dangled from his mouth and the sleeves of his white T-shirt were rolled up. Shades of James Dean in *Rebel without a Cause.*

He flexed a bicep. She laughed and stepped outside into the bright sunlight.

"Hey, baby," he said, cigarette still in his mouth. He pulled it out. "'Dream as if you'll live forever. Live as if you'll die today.'" He grinned.

He did know his James Dean.

Married. A child. Divorced. How much more did she not know about this man?

"You want to go for a spin?"

"Okay. Just let me lock up."

She ran into the shop and grabbed her keys. Back outside, Mike held open the passenger door for her. He sauntered around to slide into the driver's seat and rev the engine a couple of times.

"Impressed?" he asked.

"Not exactly." She laughed at his stricken expression.

"All this I did and I'm not making any points?" He put the car into gear and pulled away from the curb.

The breeze tousled her hair. "You're making points, don't worry. Although I'm not so sure about the cigarette…"

He pulled it from his mouth and held it out to her. Just a cylinder of rolled paper, held tight with a piece of scotch tape.

"Nice." She handed it back and hooked a thumb over her shoulder at the empty space where the backseat should have been. "I see the restoration isn't quite finished."

"Not hardly. But once we fixed the brakes and put on new tires, I couldn't resist taking her out for a ride. Especially when it's a hot summer day and there's a beautiful woman down the street I want to impress."

She tried to think of something witty to say, but was too caught up in his flattery to formulate a reply. So she settled for just smiling inanely. Mike pulled the car into the ice-cream parlor at the edge of town and picked up two chocolate milk shakes, then set off down the highway.

"So where are we going?" She sucked on the fat red straw.

"You'll see."

"Hmm. A mystery. Have I been there before?"

He pursed his lips. "Based on your age when you moved out of town, I would guess the answer is…maybe."

"And it's okay if we have milk shakes with us?"

"No problem at all."

She dropped her head back and raised her face to the glorious blue sky. The wind whipped across her cheeks and tossed her hair and she realized she hadn't experienced this feeling of freedom in a long time.

"Makes you feel like a kid again, doesn't it?" he said.

Yeah. Like she was seventeen and Mike had finally, *finally* noticed she was alive. Too bad fifteen years and a lot of water had gone under the bridge since then. Because all the naivete she'd once had about the permanence of relationships had long since washed away.

Mike reached across to put an arm around

her shoulders and pull her close. "We may as well do this right," he said.

Delaney took a draw of her milk shake. Even all that water under the bridge couldn't dampen the thrill she was getting from riding in a classic convertible with the top down and Mike's arm around her.

After several minutes Mike turned onto a narrow paved road leading into a state forest—the road to Sunset Point, the place where every teenager in the know went to park. "Figure out where we're going yet?"

"It's a little early, isn't it?" She laughed and brushed the hair off her face.

"So you *have* you been out here."

"No, I was far too chaste when I lived in Holiday Bay. And you? How much time did you spend at the point?"

"Well…" He drank his shake.

"Are you hedging?" she teased.

"No. Counting."

"Counting? As in number of girls?" She jabbed his shoulder and he laughed. "Humph. Take me home." She slid back against the passenger door and crossed her arms over her chest, feigning offense.

"Too late," he said.

They pulled out of the woods into a

parking lot along a high scenic overlook; the waters of Green Bay shimmered below them in the afternoon sun. Mike shut off the engine. "Welcome to Sunset Point. Come on." He opened his door and stepped outside, grabbing her hand and pulling her with him into the woods along no discernible path.

"Hey, Meriwether Lewis, where are we going?"

"Just follow me." He dropped her hand and picked his way through the underbrush, stepping over muddy patches and ducking below low-hanging branches. The smell of moist wood and dirt, of the spring forest in the shade, filled her senses.

Milk shake in hand, she followed Mike without speaking. After ten minutes of steady downhill hiking, they broke out of the woods onto a dirt-and-rock outcropping. She gasped.

Green Bay stretched out in front of them as expansive as a sea, the sun glittering on the deep blue surface like gems on a velvet display cloth. Far below, waves lapped gently on a narrow sand beach.

"This is incredible. How did you find it?"

Mike reached over to pull some leaves from her hair. His fingers brushed against her cheek and his eyes met hers. "Dan and I discovered it in high school."

She inhaled. "Bringing girls down here?"

He gave her a sheepish grin. "We were trying to find a path to the beach. Figured it would really impress our dates—you know, a private spot on the beach, a blanket on the sand, a bottle of cheap wine. Way more romantic than making out in the car."

He was right about that. "Did you find a path *all* the way down?"

"Gets too steep. The lake has undercut a lot of the cliff."

He sat on the rock shelf, legs stretched out in front of him. Setting his milk shake to one side, he leaned back on his hands.

"Probably didn't matter once you found this place." She tried to spot the scenic overlook, but could see nothing but rocks and trees above her.

He followed her gaze. "You can't see down here from up there. It's totally private."

"How *convenient* for high-school boys." She sat beside him, one bare knee accidentally brushing his thigh as she crossed her legs. She wanted to pull her leg away but couldn't bring herself to do it. "This hard ground, though... not real conducive to making out."

Mike put a hand on her knee. She caught her breath. "Don't tell me." She forced a light laugh.

"Yeah," he said sheepishly. "We used to keep a couple of blankets down here sealed in plastic garbage bags."

"You've got to be kidding me! You planned ahead like that?"

"We had one goal. Come on, we were seventeen-, eighteen-year-old boys."

"Nineteen, twenty…"

"Okay, guilty as charged. But I haven't brought anyone here in years. Except Andy. And she just thinks it's a fun place for a picnic that Dan and I found exploring as kids."

And me, Delaney thought. *You just brought me out here.*

He looked at her as though he'd just had the same thought. Delaney's heart began to beat faster. And then the moment stretched too long and she glanced away. "Do you ever regret moving back? Leaving Chicago?" Her hand trembled slightly as she sipped her shake, now more like warm thick chocolate milk than ice cream.

He shook his head. "It's the best place for Andy to grow up. And I like being in charge of my time. In Chicago, other people owned me. I worked for a high-profile firm doing mergers and acquisitions."

"Wow. And you don't miss the excitement of it?" She couldn't imagine never again experiencing the exhilaration she got from advertising. She shifted her leg farther away from his.

"You mean the long hours and the stress? No. When Andy's mom took a job out of the country, it seemed like the right time to make a change, simplify. My daughter was already eight years old. I wanted to be able to go to her spring recitals, be there when she 'flew up' from Brownies to Girl Scouts."

Delaney tried not to gape. "You're sounding too good to be true."

"Well, okay, I didn't really *want* to attend the fly-up ceremony. But she wanted me there, so…" He shrugged.

He still sounded too good to be true. Luckily, unlike her mother, Delaney learned early on that if something seemed too good to be true, it usually was. Especially where men were concerned.

Her mother had spent a lifetime searching for her white knight, never realizing that inside every suit of shining armor was just another mortal man who would let her down.

Delaney would never make that mistake. No matter how hard the guy made her heart pound.

"I can't even imagine leaving the advertising world," she said. "After being off work for three months, I'm chomping at the bit to get back in."

MIKE TURNED SLOWLY. "Three months? Did I miss something? You've only been here a week."

She blushed and dropped her chin. "I probably should have told you right away, but…" She shrugged. "I got laid off when my agency lost the big client I was the account executive for."

He couldn't believe it. Delaney needed this inheritance as much as the rest of them did—maybe even more. She wasn't on a leave of absence; he didn't have to romance her to get her to stay long enough to finish the weddings. He'd taken her for a drive today, brought her out to Sunset Point all as part of the plan. He'd even figured on kissing her again today. But now, he didn't have to.

He looked at her mouth, at her softly parted lips, and remembered Wednesday night in the bar. He jerked his thoughts back to the present. "I didn't realize you were out of work. That's too bad. I know some advertising guys in Green Bay I could call if you're interested."

Her eyebrows arched. "Uh, thanks. But, no, I don't think so."

"Not worldly enough, huh?"

"Oh, no. Well…yeah." She laughed self-consciously.

He'd suspected as much the first day he talked to her on the phone. Delaney McBride had big fish to fry in places far from here. She was way beyond Holiday Bay.

He considered her carefully and thought about what it had been like to kiss her, how she'd felt pressed against him, his hands in that silky hair. No. None of that mattered. He'd come home to simplify his life. And getting involved with Delaney would only add complication. Because to her, the life he'd chosen didn't look simplified. It merely looked simple.

"Ready to go back to work?" he asked.

She nodded and scrambled to her feet, leading the way into the woods. As he watched her, the realization hit him with all the force of a baseball to the head. He still wanted to kiss her.

CHAPTER SEVEN

THE HEIRS' MEETING WAS going nowhere fast. Delaney set her elbows on the library's conference table and bit her tongue for the third time in half an hour as Mike tried to get the Henrys back on track. And they ignored him again. The two men seemed to take an almost perverse delight in antagonizing each other. She was beginning to wonder whether the group might not be better off meeting somewhere public. At least then the Henrys might be embarrassed into behaving themselves.

"Stonewall, you haven't got the brains God gave wild geese." Sully gestured at the other Henry with a fat-fingered hand as though pronouncing a royal edict.

Stonewall drew his bushy brows together and crossed his arms over his chest. "When God was passing out the brains," he said in a condescending drawl, "you thought he said 'trains' and hopped a ride out of town."

"Guys," Mike said, "we need a report. What's your progress on the band shell? Are you on target to meet the deadline?"

Both men started talking at once. Mike held up a hand. "One at a time. Stonewall, you first."

"The thing is, we need to do this right. And there's not enough time for that. How are we supposed to—"

"That attitude is what's the problem," Sully said. "Every time we try to settle something, Stonewall, well, stonewalls it. What about this? What about that? He sees more road-blocks than—"

Mike stood. "Listen, guys, you have got to find a way to work together."

"I only ask questions to make sure we do this right," Stonewall shot out.

"Right? You mean right, as in *do it your way.*" Sully shook his head.

Megan cleared her throat. "You know, there's usually not a right way or a wrong way—"

"And just what's wrong with my way?"

"Okay, time-out." Mike made the referee hand signal.

Delaney stood. She appreciated the diplomacy Mike was using to get these guys to work together. She especially appreciated how hard it must be for him not to launch an F-bomb at them. But she had a wedding in just two days for which she'd just this afternoon put out a fire, and she had no time for ridiculous fighting.

"What is wrong with you two?" she demanded. Every head in the room spun to face her. "This is only our second meeting and the two of you have fought through both of them like spoiled children." Her cell phone vibrated in her pocket, but she ignored it. "I don't know what's behind all this animosity and, frankly, I don't care. We all have jobs to do. I'm doing mine. Mike and Dan are doing theirs. Do you expect me to believe that Aunt Eleanor and Uncle Henry would have appreciated you acting this way?"

She crossed her arms over her chest just as Stonewall had, feeling like the substitute teacher in front of an out-of-control class. Her cell phone vibrated again. "What I'd like to know is whether you're going to do the job or not. Because I'm not exactly loving this wedding-planning thing, and if you're not going to do your part, then I've had enough right now. Do I make myself clear?"

She could see shocked expressions all

around, Mike's included. Good. She pulled her cell phone out of her pocket to check the caller ID and was surprised to see the number for the ad agency where she used to work. It was almost 9:00 p.m. on the East Coast. Nothing unusual for that place; working late was just business as usual. But why were they calling her?

"I've got to return this call," she said. "While I'm gone, Stonewall and Sully, you figure out what you're doing. If you're planning to quit, you need to decide that now, not next month. Because if that's the case, my career as a wedding planner is over, as well. I'll expect an answer when I return."

She stalked out of the meeting room to the sound of dead silence, strode past the checkout desk and through the main door. As the last rays of the young summer sun cast their pale light on the library steps, she punched in the code to her voice mail and retrieved her messages. The scent of a nearby lilac bush in full bloom sent her right back to her childhood, to running through town barefoot, hot on Mike's heels. Her anger at the Henrys softened. They probably weren't used to tight deadlines, didn't thrive under pressure like she did.

The recorded voice of a former coworker captured her attention. "Hey, Delaney, it's Carolyn. How's the wedding planning going? You are not going to believe this—Jack had lunch with the marketing director at Avalon Cosmetics and they're not so happy with the agency they switched to. Doesn't mean they're coming back or anything, but at least you're sort of vindicated. Other than that, the same old, same old. Long hours, big presentations, low pay. Call me when you can break away from all those brides!"

Delaney replayed the message, then slowly closed her phone and leaned against the brick wall of the library. Back at the place where she belonged they were making things happen. They were kicking butt and taking names. If she were there, she'd be in brainstorming meetings, creating advertising campaigns, working long hours to pull together client proposals.

But instead, here she was in Weddingville, where, yes, she would be putting in long hours—arranging for white doves to be released at exactly the moment the church bells rang, which would ring at exactly the moment the bride said *I do*. She punched in Carolyn's number.

"They're not happy?" she said when Carolyn answered. "Did I predict this or what?"

Carolyn laughed. "You didn't hear it from me, but supposedly Jack is working 'em."

Delaney sat on the library steps. "God, would I love to be in on this."

"Who knows? If it goes anywhere, maybe you will be."

Delaney's smile came slowly. She would give just about anything to be back there and part of the action again. "Too bad I've got these weddings to plan." And brides and their mothers to keep happy. Oh, boy.

"Well, nothing's happening yet. They only had lunch today. And the marketing manager could just be stroking Jack to make him feel better about losing the account."

"Yeah, well, keep me posted."

"I'll put in a word for you if it looks like it's coming to anything."

After another few minutes of chatting, Delaney ended the call and considered everything Carolyn had told her. Realistically, it wasn't likely that Avalon would dump their new agency and go back to the old. It would be too scandalous, too much wasted time and money. And even if they did, there was no guarantee Delaney would be asked to return as account executive. Still, stranger things had happened in the world of advertising.

Overhead, pink and gold streaked the sky and she got annoyed at the beauty of it. She didn't want lovely sunsets. She wanted back into advertising.

The library door opened and she turned to see Mike stalking toward her, his mouth tight. He paused at the top of the steps. "Way to go, Dale Carnegie. How to win friends and influence people."

She huffed. She didn't want to hear a lecture about dealing with the Henrys.

"It just took me ten minutes to undo the damage you caused and get the Henrys to keep working together. You have no idea how hard it was to get them to agree to do this in the first place." He dropped down beside her.

She forced herself not to move away from him. Her world was crappy enough right now; she didn't need Mike telling her how bad she was and making it worse. "They cause their own damage."

"Those two guys lost one of their best friends."

"Years ago."

"No matter. They were a threesome."

"I know all about it. The 3-H Club—cello, violin and piano."

"No, they were more than that—golf, poker, fishing, you name it. Then Henry Clark died. And that left these two, who never got along very well in the first place."

"So now they hate each other? That doesn't make sense."

"Everybody grieves in their own way and time, Pumpkin." He patted her knee and she clenched her jaw at the patronizing gesture.

"All I know is it's Thursday night," she said evenly. "And I've got an even bigger wedding to pull off this weekend than last."

"And all *I* know is if we want to get our inheritances, we can't go around pissing each other off. So let me give you a piece of wisdom learned from my years in law. You can catch more flies with honey than with vinegar."

An acid-laced retort leaped to the tip of her tongue, but before she could let loose with it, he was already standing.

"Now, Pumpy, let's go finish the meeting because I'm sure everyone's getting restless in there."

Pumpy? *Pumpy?* She'd had enough of being Pumpy. She'd had enough of trying to figure out why he'd never gotten past the fat redhead she used to be. Who did he think he was?

She stood and leveled a cold stare on him. "No, Mikey, I don't think so. I don't need your lectures, I don't need your sympathy, I don't need your rah-rah cheerleading." Suddenly, she realized, she wasn't sure she even liked this adult Mike at all. Maybe she'd never liked who he was, just the image of who she wanted him to be. How could she even have thought herself attracted to him? "And I really don't need to be Pumpy McBride anymore. Have you ever given any thought to what it felt like—feels like—to be called Pumpkin when you're red-haired and fat?"

He stared at her.

"No. I didn't think so." Oh, this felt good. "Frankly, I've had quite enough of tonight's heirs' meeting if you don't mind." She took off down the sidewalk purposefully, covering long stretches of concrete with her strides, knowing that Mike was watching her go. *Let him watch my back. Let him watch me walk right out of this town and out of his life.* She tossed her hair dramatically.

Not that she was in his life anyway. And not that she could leave this town before the weddings were done and her inheritance secured. Her steps faltered and slowed. She felt as if she was in a movie and any minute the hero should chase her down the sidewalk and stop her, tell her how sorry he was and beg her to stay.

But at the end of the second block, she resigned herself to the fact that life just wasn't that well scripted. And this town sure as hell was no movie set.

Head down, hands in her jacket pockets, she hurried toward the wedding shop. Much as she wanted to chuck wedding planning for the night, she knew she'd better stop in and check her messages. She'd been out since midafternoon with last-minute appointments: watching the bride hang on for dear life while practicing riding sidesaddle at Lucky C Stables in preparation for Saturday's ceremony; meeting with the restaurant manager to confirm the seating and menu for the rehearsal dinner; clearing up confusion at the bakery about a supposed cancellation of the cake order... Luckily, she'd taken care of that mistake without much trouble.

Still, with a bride she'd privately taken to calling Bridezilla, this event would be nothing if not a challenge.

She stepped into the office and pointed a finger at the red light blinking on the answering machine. "I forbid you to be anything but good news." Pen in hand, she settled into the desk chair and hit Play, fully expecting yet another frantic call from the bride-to-be. Sunday morning couldn't come fast enough.

"Hi, Delaney," an older woman said. "This is Karen at Floral Fantasies. It's Thursday about five. I hate to leave this on the answering machine, but I've tried to call you a couple of times already…" Her serious tone made Delaney uneasy.

"We've had something of a disaster."

Delaney's stomach began to churn.

"When I came in this morning, I discovered our cooler had malfunctioned and our flowers, everything we had, froze. All our roses, carnations and daisies. All those lovely calla lilies and orchids ruined. I didn't call you because the wholesaler said they could deliver replacements today. But I've just received the order and—" Karen drew an audible breath "—the orchids are the wrong color and the callas aren't there. Since it's June, I can't even get enough of the blooms your bride wants at the Milwaukee wholesaler. Too many other weddings…" The woman's voice quivered. "I can get a lot of different flowers right away, just not all the ones she wanted. Maybe the bride would be okay with something else. Please give me a call as soon as you get this. I'll keep trying to reach you."

The machine clicked off and Delaney slowly set the pen on the pad of paper. Tears leaped to her eyes and she squeezed them back. The wedding was at one o'clock, the day after tomorrow. Now she had thirty-six hours to figure out the flowers? How could she call this bride and ask if she'd take something else? She hadn't nicknamed the woman Bridezilla because she was easy to work with.

She hit Play again, then slumped in her chair and closed her eyes.

MIKE STOOD IN THE doorway to the shop's office and watched Delaney as the message played. Watched the soft light from the desk lamp highlight the golden strands in her red hair. He'd known from the moment he'd first heard her on the phone that Pumpkin McBride had grown up. But he'd never taken the time to consider the woman she'd become—and what she had gone through to get there. Not when Dan proposed he romance Pumpkin to keep her in town. Not even when he reluctantly agreed to do it. And especially not minutes ago when he'd treated her like a wayward child in need of his expert guidance.

"Hey, Delaney?"

She jerked her head up and punched the off button on the answering machine. "How does everyone get in this store without jangling the bell?"

He shrugged apologetically.

"Aren't you supposed to be at the heirs' meeting?" she asked.

"We adjourned early again. Seem to have a real problem finishing those meetings." He stepped into the room. "I just wanted to say I'm sorry. And if you don't want my lectures or my sympathy or my cheerleading, much as it breaks my heart, I understand." He smiled sheepishly. "And, well, how about if I never call you Pumpkin again?"

She looked at him for what felt like a full minute. "That would be a start."

"And I'll never give you advice again, unless you ask for it."

She just looked at him, her expression unreadable. "And you'll never bring up vinegar and honey."

"Never."

"Or Dale Carnegie," she said.

"Or Dale Carnegie."

"Or any derivative of Pumpkin."

"Or any derivative of Pumpkin," he said quietly.

She nodded and looked away.

"We never meant any harm. Not then. Not now. Pumpkin was mostly because of the red hair. Just like they called me 007 because my last name was Connery. And Dan was Hobes because his last name was Hobart. And Jack Turleton was Spike—"

"Because of his grandstanding in the football games. Yeah, I know. I get it. All the guys had nicknames. All the guys and me, the fat redhead."

"No. Just *the redhead.* So what do you say, Delaney? Will you forgive me if I promise never to screw up again?"

In the subdued light, he saw the vulnerability in her expression and for just a second, the young girl whose heart had always been big enough to forgive the transgressions against her. And then the girl was gone. Delaney rolled her eyes and stuck out a hand. "Don't get carried away. You're a man. You'll screw up again."

"What? Delaney, you cut me to the quick."

He clasped her hand and she flashed him a quick grin. And he realized all he wanted to do was pull her into his arms and kiss her. He waved at the answering machine and dropped into the extra chair beside her desk. "Let's hear that message again."

Delaney played it twice more as though the mere sound of it might provide a solution. Then she called the florist. Mike couldn't help admiring how she took charge of the conversation, searching for an answer even though it was clear there was no quick fix.

She hung up the phone, shaking her head. "I don't know how my aunt handled the stress. In just two weddings I've already had three crises. The singer got laryngitis. Then the cake fiasco. And now this. That's not even taking into consideration what it's like dealing with the brides. God knows what lies ahead."

"What cake fiasco?"

"You'll enjoy this," Delaney said. "I stopped in the bakery today to confirm they'd be bringing an assortment of petit fours along with the cake. Somehow they thought we'd canceled the cake. Said someone called."

"Why would anyone cancel the wedding cake?"

"That's what *I* said. Obviously they got

the orders mixed up. Anyway, everything's fine. We'll have a cake Saturday."

Mike let his head drop back against the chair. "I'm feeling your wedding-planning pain. What's the verdict with the flowers? Listening to your end of the phone call, I got the impression the only option was to fly them in from a tropical island."

"Close. We can get everything from a wholesaler in Chicago. But they can't deliver until end of workday tomorrow."

Mike ran a hand through his hair. "Way too late. Doesn't leave time to arrange them."

"Right. Karen would pick them up, but she's got too many orders to redo for other events."

"How about talking the bride into changing her flowers?"

"Bridezilla? Not a chance. If I force this on her, it would pretty much guarantee an unsatisfactory rating."

"Game over." He picked up a pencil from Delaney's desktop and twirled it in his fingers as he contemplated their options.

"The wholesaler opens at 7:00 a.m. If I leave here at 1:00 a.m., I can be there when the doors open."

"And drive back on no sleep?" he asked.

"Ever hear of caffeine?"

"Ever hear of falling asleep at the wheel?" he said. "Or breaking down? The side of the highway at three in the morning is not a good place for a woman alone."

Delaney stood and began to pace the small office. "I told Karen I could help arrange the flowers. But I have to get them here first."

She wasn't listening to him. "How about using a delivery service?" he suggested.

"Yeah, except to get the flowers here by noon would probably cost a fortune. And with my luck, something would go wrong. I'm sure Karen would let me use the Floral Fantasies van." She stopped and looked at him. "I'm going to Chicago. Tonight."

"I'll go with you."

"No need. You've got legal things to do tomorrow." She gave him a backhanded wave.

"This is more important. And we'll be home by noon, anyway." As she began to shake her head, he held up a hand. "No arguments. Andy's at my folks. I'll swing over there and make sure she can stay overnight. You get the van. I'll meet you back here at one."

SOMETIME AFTER FOUR in the morning, Delaney steered the old white van onto the Milwaukee bypass. Lights flashed across the windows as she passed the few other cars on the highway and the brightly lit signs of stores and restaurants that had closed hours ago. The van felt like a cocoon, a haven against the emptiness just outside its doors.

She drank some coffee from her insulated mug and peeked over at Mike, asleep, curled into a pillow against the door. She was glad he'd insisted on coming along; it was reassuring not to be alone, to have someone else, another driver, with her.

She let herself remember what it was like to kiss him, wondered what it would be like to wake up with him in the morning, have him roll over and wrap her in his arms and kiss her to consciousness.

Her headlights lit up a police car hidden under an overpass, exposing the radar gun in its window. It seemed as if everything and everyone had something they were trying to hide, she thought. Sometimes you just had to look deeper to discover what it was.

Like her mother. After she died, Delaney had found twelve brand-new dresses in her mother's closet. She tightened her grip on the steering wheel. Twelve elegant pastel dresses, each with the tags still on, each bought by her mother to get remarried in, a new dress every time she thought she'd met the man of her dreams. Twelve dresses that exposed her mother's desperation, revealed a lifetime spent searching for a man to rely on and belong with—and never finding him.

Mike's cell phone blared the William Tell Overture from deep in the pocket where he'd stashed it and he jerked awake. He dug the phone out and cleared his throat as he flipped it open. "Hello?" A moment later he said, "Cassie, it's like—" he focused on the dash-board clock "—four-thirty in the morning."

Who was Cassie?

"That's because I'm *not* at home. I'm driving to Chicago." A pause and then, "Because I need to be there at seven in the morning. Everything's fine. Andy's at my parents'. I never got your message because I only went home for a few minutes tonight and didn't check the machine." He sat silent, listening, then said, "I'm sure she'll be excited. You'll be back for how long?"

Delaney locked her hands on the steering wheel. Was this Andy's mom? Mike's former wife?

"You can tell her yourself. She'll be home after three." By the tone of Mike's voice, he was trying to wrap up the call. "Okay, yeah,

I'll tell her." He sounded disappointed. "Yeah. Thanks for calling. Bye." He closed the phone and slouched back into the pillow.

"My ex-wife," he said. "In Berlin. It's six hours later there."

"I take it she was worried?"

He shrugged. "I guess. She's coming back for the first two weeks of August and wanted to tell Andy."

"Andy will be excited, I'm sure."

"Yeah, but God forbid she interrupt whatever function she had tomorrow to call Andy after school and give her the news herself."

"Maybe she doesn't have a choice." Delaney knew what it was like to have a demanding job.

"I guess. She's a pretty high-powered attorney. Important."

Delaney could hear the lack of respect in his voice.

Mike shifted his position against the door. "We were law students when we met—and stupid. She got pregnant. We married. Graduated law school. Passed the bar exam. Got jobs. Had a baby." His voice softened. "Started making a life together."

Envy quietly seeped into Delaney. She knew the answer to her next question even before she asked it. "Did you love her?"

"Yeah. I loved her a lot."

She reached a hand toward him and he grasped it. "I'm so sorry. I wish it had worked out for you," she said, meaning it. Regardless of what she believed, she actually did wish love would work out for someone.

"Cassie used to say if she wanted to get to the top, she had to put in twice the hours as anyone else in the office."

"That's kind of what women are up against." She knew it well.

Delaney changed lanes to pass a lone car on the highway. Now that they were past the city with its overhead lights and neon signs, the night seemed darker, the sky lower.

Mike took an Oreo cookie from the package on the floor, twisted it apart and put half in his mouth. "I came home from work one day to find Andy in her high chair eating Cheerios and Cassie at the kitchen table drinking a martini with three fat olives on the swizzle stick. As we talked, every time she made an important point, she sucked down one of those olives."

"You don't have to tell me this."

"It's okay." He jammed the rest of the Oreo into his mouth. "Olive number one— she didn't love me, we never should have married just because she was pregnant. Olive number two—she was leaving. And olive number three…" He paused. "I could have custody of the baby."

Delaney let out a gasp. A lump welled up in her throat at his and Andy's loss. "How did you stand it?"

He shrugged. "I got this great kid out of the deal. We're a pretty good team. The rest? You just file it away. What other choice is there? Some things it's best not to think about."

Delaney watched the broken white center line as though it were a path she was supposed to follow, an unchanging path with no beginning and no end, leading to God knew where. For Mike, it had led him away from the pain of his marriage and back to Holiday Bay. For her, it was an arrow pointing directly toward Boston.

She took the next off-ramp, pulled into a gas station and filled up the tank. It was Mike's turn to drive. She needed to sleep. Because sleep was the only way she'd be able keep from dwelling on the fact that Mike had never gotten over his ex-wife.

CHAPTER EIGHT

BACK IN HOLIDAY BAY, Delaney dropped Mike off at his car and sped over to the florist shop. Karen hurried out the front door, her short gray hair messy, as if she hadn't combed it in about two days. "You made it!" she said. "I tried not to worry about whether there'd be any more problems. Just worked hard all morning, so everything else is caught up." She pulled open the back doors of the van. "They had everything we ordered?"

"Ready and waiting when we got there. We double-checked before we left."

"And you can still help?" Karen picked up a box of flowers and led the way to the cooler.

"I can't claim any experience or skill, but the hands and mind are willing. All night if we have to, just as long as these flowers are ready before morning."

"It shouldn't take *all* night." Karen smiled and her face creased into rows of soft folds.

"Wonderful. Because I'm feeling a little sleep-deprived right now." Delaney yawned and set her box on the cooler floor. She shivered. "It's downright freezing in here."

"Not quite freezing. Forty degrees. That's what I keep it at." Karen pointed at a thermostat on the wall right inside the door. "There's the culprit."

"The cause of all our troubles." Delaney shivered. "Seventy-five degrees outside and forty in here." She followed Karen outside to get the rest of the boxes. When they'd finished unloading, she asked, "Does that happen often? That the thermostat malfunctions?"

Karen stilled. "Never. Not once in all my years of being in business. But, as with everything, there's always a first time." She collected an assortment of calla lilies, roses and orchids and brought them out of the cooler to the butcher block worktable. "Now, I'll put together one of the centerpieces as a sample to follow. Then you can get started." She opened a box filled with identical clear vases and took out several.

Delaney frowned. "So did they say what caused the problem? It couldn't happen again, could it?"

"It won't happen again because nothing

was wrong with it. Somehow, it got turned down. Now here's what you do…" She quickly demonstrated how to trim the stems at a forty-five-degree angle under running water and arrange them in the vase with ferns and baby's breath. "Voilà! It's a work of art," she said, standing back to view her creation.

Delaney had tried to pay attention but she was too busy trying to wrap her brain around the fact that *somehow* the thermostat got turned down. "That simple, huh?"

"That's right. You'll need to put together thirty-five of those. I'll get started on the bridesmaids' bouquets."

"Okay." Delaney picked up a purple orchid. She had to make thirty-five center-pieces on a couple of hours of sleep? She had to make thirty-five centerpieces that looked *professional* on a couple of hours of sleep? These were going to be *stunning*. She cut the orchid's stem and set it into one of the vases. That was pretty. She added another orchid, then trimmed a white calla lily and slid that in, too. Not bad. How about some baby's breath? Fabulous. She patted the flowers in the vase lovingly. "So I'm just wondering, if nothing was wrong with the thermostat, how would it get turned down?"

Karen shook her head. "You saw where it's located. I must have nudged it when I was carrying something in or out. Need to be more careful." The woman's fingers fairly flew as she wrapped floral tape about the stems of callas and roses. "Making a bouquet is like making a larger version of a corsage," she said. "And a corsage is often just three boutonnieres put together. Once you finish the centerpieces, I'll show you how to make the boutonnieres."

Delaney blanched. At the rate she was going, she wouldn't be starting boutonnieres until midnight. She picked up the pace. "But you've never nudged it before?"

Karen's eyebrows pulled together in confusion.

"The thermostat. You've never nudged it before?"

"No. But I've never been this busy before, either. I had to prepare for three weddings and a retirement party this weekend." She hot-glued a light blue ribbon around the flower stems she'd just taped. "I think bouquets look better when the stems are showing, so I always let them stick out the bottom of the ribbon." She tied a multilooped bow at the base and held up the finished product.

"Gorgeous," Delaney said absently. She couldn't stop thinking about the conversation she'd overheard at last weekend's wedding. She trimmed some calla lilies and set them in the vase. "Is it possible someone meant to turn the temperature down a few degrees and then accidentally did too much?" As she waited for Karen's answer, the blood began to pound in her ears.

"No one touches the thermostat. It needs to be at forty degrees. No reason to change it."

Delaney allowed herself a small smile. She'd bet her glass slippers that something was not quite right in Holiday Bay. And she was going to get to the bottom of it. "You don't think someone could have turned the cooler down on purpose, do you?"

Karen raised her head, eyes wide. "Why would anyone do that?"

Delaney made a lame gesture with an orchid. "I don't know… Sabotage? Is there anyone who might want to ruin your flowers? And so…turn down the thermostat to do that?"

Karen wrapped a wire around the stems of another bridesmaid's bouquet and didn't answer.

"I'm not accusing anyone," Delaney said

hastily. "I've probably just watched too many movies."

"You're sounding a bit like my husband. He wants me to put a lock on the thermostat now."

Delaney inhaled softly. Validation. Let Mike laugh at her conspiracy theory now. "Was there anyone new in the store Wednesday? Anyone acting strangely?" She pretended to be concentrating on arranging flowers.

Karen stopped to think. "I don't entirely remember who was here. You know how one day blends into the next, especially at my age. I suppose I could check my receipts."

Thank God, let's check the receipts!

Karen went into the office and pulled a stack of pages from a file drawer. She began to flip through them, thinking out loud. "No. No. Not her. Not her, either. Not him—"

"Wait a minute. Tell me who you're talking about. You may be too close to this to be objective."

Karen pursed her lips. "This first one is another bride whose wedding is tomorrow. It surely wouldn't be her." She held up a receipt. "And this, this is Robert's Real Estate. They order flowers every week for their open houses." She ran through a couple of other customers who didn't appear to have any connection to the will or Delaney's aunt.

"Anyone else?"

"Dan Hobart was in that day."

"Dan?" Surely he wouldn't have tried to undermine her success. Not Dan.

"Flowers for his wife. Said they'd finished their birthing classes and he wanted to send her an arrangement to celebrate. Isn't that sweet?"

Delaney nodded. "Dan wouldn't have turned down the thermostat. Anyone else?"

"There's a few more." Karen flipped through the remaining receipts. "Your uncle Lou stopped in."

"My uncle?" Delaney thought her heart was going to stop beating right then and there. Hide in plain sight—or something like that. "What did he want?"

"Ordered a plant to be sent as an anniversary gift." She examined the receipt more closely. "And Claire got a spring bouquet for the office—I made it up on the spot."

Her uncle had opportunity. And motive. Even though she'd thrown his name out to Mike last weekend, she hadn't truly believed he would do anything to undermine her success. He may have always been a loner fixated on making money, but she had trouble believing he would be so devious. "Is that it, then, for Wednesday? No other customers?"

Karen showed her two other receipts of people who didn't appear to have any connection to Aunt Ellie. "I'm just a small shop, so you see why it's hard for me to believe... I mean, who of these people would want to hurt my business?"

"I don't know. Maybe you did accidentally nudge the dial." Delaney squeezed her hands into fists. And maybe her uncle knew exactly what he was doing when he came in here that day. Working to get an inheritance.

MIKE SAT FORWARD on the couch and checked the time on his cell phone. Nine forty-five. Delaney had said she'd call when they were done making bouquets; obviously they were still working. Earlier, he'd offered to help, but she assured him they had everything in control, no assistance necessary. "This is harder than it looks," she said. "By the time you learn, we'll be done. Besides, I've got to break for the rehearsal."

So here he sat in front of the TV, half watching *The Terminator.* Great movie. Just not what he wanted to be doing right now. He reached into the oversize bag of chocolate-covered peanuts on the couch next to him, grabbed a handful and dropped several into his mouth. Andy was sleeping at a friend's house. Dan and Megan were at home, hoping labor would begin any minute. And though he knew he could go down to Ollie's and see any number of acquaintances, he didn't want to. After last night in the car, he wanted to spend more time with Delaney. He'd ostensibly called to check on her progress with the flowers, but the truth was, he wanted to see her—even though she was a complication he didn't need. Even though this could end up being one step forward, two steps back.

He tried to concentrate on the movie, closing his eyes as he recited some of the lines along with the actors. Then he let thoughts of Delaney block everything else out and he drifted toward sleep.

The ringing of his cell phone jarred him to full consciousness, and he jerked upright in confusion. He glanced at the time on his phone before flipping it open. Ten-thirty? He'd fallen asleep? He stifled a yawn. "Hello?"

"Flowers all done," Delaney said in a cheery voice. "Don't tell me you were sleeping."

"No, no. Just watching TV. You're finished,

huh? And the rehearsal? That went okay, too?" He knew he sounded semicoherent.

"The flowers are beautiful. The rehearsal went fine, right according to plan."

"Busy night."

"And I still have to run down to the beach to make sure the tent and lights are set up, and the chairs and tables have been delivered. Just want to make a quick check in case there are any obvious issues."

"Not a lot of time in the morning for last-minute inspections," he said.

"Exactly."

There was an enthusiasm in her voice he found really appealing. "You sound awfully energetic after driving all night, working on flowers all day and coordinating a wedding rehearsal."

"Amazing, isn't it? No. I just had a shower and washed away the fatigue. Presto-change-o, I'm completely awake. I suppose once I sit down it'll hit me like a ton of bricks. I hope so, anyway." She laughed and the sound slid over him like a soft caress. "Otherwise, I'll be the zombie stumbling around the wedding."

"Sounds like an appropriate guest for Bridezilla's event."

Delaney laughed again. "I guess I'd better get going…"

"Need any help?"

"No, I should be okay."

Mike hung up and thought about Delaney out on the beach, alone in the dark. Of course she'd be okay. She was used to driving her own train. Knowing her, though, she might stay there half the night fine-tuning things. And if she was going to be on top of her game tomorrow, she really needed to get some sleep. So did he, but that catnap he just took would keep him awake for hours.

He wandered into the kitchen and opened the refrigerator. A beer might make him tired. *A beer might make Delaney tired.*

He pulled out a six-pack of Spotted Cow, hefted it in one hand and debated the merits of swinging by the beach. Then, without consciously making a decision, he stuck a bottle opener in his pocket, scooped up his keys from the kitchen table, slipped his feet into flip-flops and strode out the door.

Ten minutes later, he'd parked at the beach and was heading across the sand, six-pack in one hand and a couple of blankets from the trunk in the other. The beam of a flashlight flickered under the big white tent in front of him and he had fleeting second thoughts. What would Delaney think, him showing up with a six-pack of beer?

What the hell. He made his way toward the flashlight beam, feet sinking into the soft still-warm sand. Suddenly, bright light hit him full in the face and he put up a hand to shield his eyes. He blinked several times.

"Mike! You about scared me to death! What are you doing out here?" Delaney lowered her flashlight. She walked toward him in formfitting gray sweatpants and a tight T-shirt, her hair in loose ringlets around her face, still damp from her shower.

He could just set all this stuff down and take her into his arms right now and kiss her senseless. His breathing sped up. "You need to quit work for the day. Figured maybe a beer or two would help you unwind so you can get some sleep."

She smiled at him. "That's so nice. Thanks. Just one more thing I want to check."

He followed her across the beach and tried not to notice her trim little butt in those tight sweatpants, tried not to wonder whether she had on underpants, because she sure as hell wasn't wearing a bra. He pictured Delaney in the shower, the water running like a silken sheet over her flushed face, her breasts, her belly, her— He swallowed hard. This was Pumpkin McBride he was having lascivious thoughts about. Pumpy.

No.

Delaney.

Oh, hell.

She stopped and shone the flashlight into the woods along the edge of the sand. "This is where the bride is supposed to get on a white horse and ride to the groom. But ever since the rehearsal, I've been thinking we need to start farther back, so no one gets a glimpse of her until she rides into view."

"You had the horse here tonight?"

"No. We just did a walk-through. Guess I'll make this change tomorrow when the horse and its handler arrive."

She looked at him and grinned and he wanted to run a finger over her lips and follow it with his mouth.

"Okay, I'm ready for a beer, even though I still have important things to do tonight." She aimed the flashlight beam down the beach.

"Like what?"

"Like iron an outfit for tomorrow. I'll be nervous enough in the morning without having to worry about what to wear."

"Think of how relaxed you'll be ironing with a beer or two under your belt. What time's the wedding again?" Mike laid out one of the blankets and tossed the other in the sand.

Delaney sat cross-legged and flipped off the flashlight; he settled beside her and waited for his eyes to adjust to the muted light cast by the half moon.

"One o'clock," she said. "But the hospitality service is coming early to set up the bar, the dance floor, the tables, that kind of stuff. And the florist will be here to decorate the aisle and set up the wedding arbor. I'm meeting everyone about eight."

"Then we won't stay too late." Mike popped the caps off two bottles and handed one to Delaney. He tapped her beer with his. "To your success in the wedding-planning business."

"Thanks. I'll need it for this all-day affair. Ceremony and pictures. Hors d'oeuvres and champagne. Dinner at four, a band, dancing…" She took a swallow of beer. "I just hope everything comes off okay."

"It will. You're getting good at this. And you're learning from an expert—your aunt." He brought his bottle to his mouth.

"Speaking of my aunt, you're never going to guess what happened at the florist today.

In fact, you'll probably want to apologize for ever doubting me. You may even go so far as to say, 'Delaney, you're brilliant.'"

"I can't wait to hear this."

Delaney recounted the discussion she'd had with Karen about the thermostat. "Two guesses as to who was in the shop the day the thermostat got turned down."

"Tiny Tim?"

Her brow furrowed.

"You know, all those tulips."

"Try again," she said in a droll voice.

He mulled it over for a few seconds. "I don't know. Eliza Doolittle?"

Delaney smacked him on the arm. "I don't think I'll even tell you." She lifted her chin and looked out over the lake.

He laughed. "Come on. I'm sorry. Tell me. *Please?*"

She leaned toward him and he could smell the scent of shampoo in her hair.

"My uncle Lou. What do you think of that, Mr. Nonbeliever?"

"Your uncle? Still thinking conspiracy theory?" he asked, more to force his brain away from thoughts about Delaney *sans* underwear and smelling so wonderful, and less because he cared whether she was into conspiracy theories.

"All I know is that last weekend I overheard someone saying that if Storybook Weddings had a few more problems the handwriting would be on the wall. Then suddenly the flowers froze. My uncle had motive. And now we know he had opportunity."

"But he doesn't have *need* and I don't think he has the personality for it, either."

Delaney sighed. "Yeah, I know. I hate even thinking this about him, anyway."

"You can't discount coincidence. Truth can be stranger than fiction." Mike finished his beer and opened two more, handing one to Delaney.

"But the thermostat got turned down. And the cake got mysteriously canceled."

"And the singer got laryngitis."

"Don't be silly."

"I'm not," Mike said. "I'm just pointing out that things happen." He paused. "Okay, let's suppose something underhanded is going on. Did your uncle go into the cooler?"

"Karen was too busy to notice." Delaney set her empty back into the cardboard holder and took a drink of the full bottle Mike had just passed her.

"So we don't actually know if your uncle had opportunity. I hate to say it, but I don't think there's enough here to mean anything."

"You're probably right."

They stared out at the bay in silence, each finishing another bottle, then opening the last two. Mike didn't know what to believe about her uncle, didn't even want to consider that in the midst of everything, they might have a rat. He breathed in the fresh air, the scent of water and sand and felt every muscle in his body loosen. He thought he'd survived their all-night drive without any lasting effects, but he was tired, after all. Delaney shifted next to him, stretched her legs out in front of her and leaned back on one hand. He could feel the warmth of her leg against his. He tried to concentrate on conspiracy theories, but the only thing he could think of was kissing Delaney. Laying her down in the sand and kissing her.

DELANEY RAN HER FINGERS through her hair to work out some of the knots the breeze had caused. She savored the cold beer as it slipped down her throat. "I think I have too active an imagination," she said. "Must come from being in advertising."

"Don't tell me all that stuff in commercials isn't true."

"It's all true, believe me." She chuckled.

"Hey, thanks for coming out here tonight. Who knows how much bigger I might have made this conspiracy by tomorrow, otherwise? Besides, this downtime is just what I needed and I'm not sure going back to my wedding-strewn apartment would have done the trick."

The breeze shifted off the lake and the temperature dropped a few degrees. She shivered.

"Cold?" Mike asked.

"Just a little."

He opened the extra blanket and wrapped it around her shoulders, pulling the ends together under her chin. His thumb brushed across her jaw and gently turned her head around to face him. Mike was looking at her in a way he never had before. In the pale moonlight, his eyes were narrowed and black. Her insides clutched. He pulled her close, until their mouths were just inches apart and she could feel his heat.

"I'm not so cold anymore," she chirped, staring at his mouth because she wasn't quite sure what to make of him and sure as hell not wanting to get caught in those eyes again. His fingers curled into her hair, caressed the back of her head and she knew she had to say something, anything. She raised her eyes tentatively to ask what this was about, but couldn't get her mouth to form the words.

Now. Say something now.

And just when she decided that the way out was to drink more beer and was lifting her bottle, he slanted his mouth across hers and took possession of her lips as if he'd owned them for a lifetime.

This was a kiss between lovers. She knew it. He knew it. *And she had a bottle of beer in her hand.*

He deepened the kiss, pulled her up against him, his hands cradling her head as he kissed her hard. He tasted of beer and then he just tasted of Mike and she couldn't get enough of him.

He kissed her throat, trailed kisses over her jaw and she let her head drop back, shivering beneath his touch.

"Lose the beer," he muttered. "It's cramping our style."

She laughed and tossed the bottle away.

Mike shifted their positions so they were lying side by side, their legs entwined, his hands skimming the soft skin of her stomach.

She pushed up on one elbow. "What…?" she said as she tried to catch her breath. "What is this all about?"

He rolled onto his back and looked at her from beneath heavily lidded eyes. He cupped her cheek with his hand and she leaned into his palm. "I don't exactly know. Do you need an explanation?"

She thought about it, then shrugged. "It's just, I'm Pumpkin…"

"Honey, you are so far from Pumpkin, I'm about to lose my mind."

She ran her hand down the strong muscles of his arm. He wrapped her fingers in his, then brought her hand to his mouth and pressed a kiss to her palm. "You are a beautiful, intelligent woman."

He drew a hand over her T-shirt across her breasts, teased her through the fabric until she couldn't take much more.

"I can't figure out why it took me so long to figure it out." He pulled her on top of him and kissed her again, and she loved the way his hard body felt against hers, and the way his hands touched her, the way she was touching him.

"Slow learner," she said, and he laughed and pulled her shirt up and over her head and rolled her onto her back. He kissed her breasts and moved a hand across her lower back to cup her rear end and pull her tight against him. She could feel his need, mirroring her own. "Although…I could be wrong about the slow-learner part," she said.

He grinned mischievously. "I think you'd be more comfortable with those pants off." He slid his hands beneath the elastic waistband of her sweatpants. And she let him. She gave herself up to his kiss, knowing that if nothing else came of her time as a wedding planner, at least she would know she'd opened and closed every door she'd ever wanted. And if it wasn't enough, well, it would have to be. Because, just like any good business decision, she knew what her options were, she knew what the consequences were of each choice, and she was willing to take the risk associated with this one.

CHAPTER NINE

HEAVY WITH SLEEP, Delaney stretched out on her side and let her thoughts drift in the nirvana between unconscious and awake. She couldn't believe how well she'd slept last night. She pulled the fleece blanket over her bare shoulders like a shield against the damp air, and let the soft sounds of the surf lull her to consciousness.

The surf?

She opened one eye to the gray early-morning light. A seagull stood not five feet away from her. A seagull in her bedroom?

The bird flapped its wings and flew away, and Delaney opened both eyes, now fully awake. She wasn't in her bed—she was on the beach. She'd stayed all night on the beach...

God help her.

Slowly, she pushed up on one elbow and turned her head. Mike was sleeping on his back next to her, one arm bent up over his face, not a sign of tension marring his features.

I made love with Mike last night. She cringed, remembering. On the beach. They'd rolled around on a blanket in the sand like teenagers until who-knew-when in the morning and then fallen asleep, dead to the world. And hadn't awakened until the sun was up.

She watched Mike's chest rise and fall and it took everything she had not to touch him, not to lay her mouth on his and wake him with a kiss, not to press her body to his, make love with him again, make him hers.

Make him hers? He would never be hers. No matter how wonderfully relationships began, they never lasted. She had to get out of here. A seagull squawked overhead and she followed its flight with her eyes, watched it land down the beach to fight over something with another gull.

She didn't want to make Mike hers, anyway, didn't want to take that path. What had she been thinking last night? She'd told herself she was opening one door so she could close another, that making love with Mike just this once would allow her to let go of her infatuation. Except… She looked at Mike and felt an ache in her chest. She hadn't closed the door at all, only left it hanging open, banging in the wind.

She pulled her arm out from under the blanket and checked her watch. Six-fifteen. She needed to get out of here before the joggers and dog walkers started showing up. Before the hospitality-service workers arrived. Before she had to face Mike.

Pressing the blanket to her chest, she picked her clothes out of the sand and gave them a shake. Well, wouldn't these be comfy to wear? Lying on her back, she wriggled them on under the blanket, conscious every moment of Mike's naked body next to her.

She looked at him again. Much as she wanted to escape, she couldn't just leave him here, sleeping. She nudged his shoulder. "Mike! Wake up!"

Yawning, he opened his eyes a crack. "Morning, beautiful," he said sleepily. "What're you doing?" He ran a hand down her arm and she shivered from his touch.

"We stayed all night." She gestured toward the bay. "It's past six. I have to get out of here before the workers start arriving."

Mike rubbed his eyes and sat up. He tossed back the blanket and reached for his shorts and T-shirt. "All night, huh?"

Delaney's chest tightened at the sight of him completely uncovered. *Get away from him. Now.* She stood and stepped toward the water, scanning the beach where the reception tent had been set up. No one was there. And only two cars were in the parking lot—hers and Mike's. Though she didn't expect the workers or the florist for well over an hour, it would be just her luck they'd want to get an early start.

She raised her face skyward. The wind was light and the temperature already warming; it would be a gorgeous day for the wedding. She ran her fingers through her tangled hair. That's what she got for letting it dry au naturel while she played around in the sand. Using both hands, she tried to work out the knots and force her hair into the semblance of a style.

From behind her she heard Mike laugh. "Hey, Medusa, I think it might be hopeless."

She whirled round and feigned offense. "Medusa?"

"I just call it like I see it." He shook off the blankets and grinned at her, all cute and fresh from sleep, his dark hair falling on his forehead, those blue eyes trying to dance their way into her heart.

She pulled her gaze away. She wasn't going to get sucked into this again, wasn't going to let her emotions get involved when she knew exactly where it would lead. Where it always led. Nowhere.

Mike came up beside her, the six-pack of empties in one hand, the blankets in the other. He looked puzzled. "Okay, let's go."

They walked across the beach in silence, every step leading them farther away from where they'd been last night. She couldn't want him. It was as simple as that. And every step they took made her more convinced that she was making the right decision.

THIS WASN'T EXACTLY HOW Mike had pictured the morning after. The warm, responsive woman he'd been with last night had completely disappeared. So much for waking in the wee hours and tucking his body around hers, the two of them slipping back to sleep entwined. Maybe Delaney was just jittery about the wedding. He touched her arm. "Hey, don't worry. You'll do great today."

Her smile was tight. "I hope so."

"By this time tomorrow, it'll be over. And within a few days, you'll have another satisfactory rating."

They reached the parking lot and stopped at Delaney's silver BMW. "It was fun last night," Mike said.

She nodded and unlocked the car door.

"I'll call you," he said. "Maybe we can take the Chevy out to Sunset Point again."

She shook her head. "It was the beer, Mike. Liquor does that to people." She waved her keys. "And exhaustion. All night driving to Chicago and back. Catching catnaps in the car. You going to work all afternoon. Me doing flowers and the wedding rehearsal. And then there was the moon and the water and the sand. Well, what would you expect? I mean, what would anyone expect?"

He loved how she gestured with her hands when she got agitated. "What are you talking about?"

"Fatigue. It caused the beer to go straight to our heads, released our inhibitions and made us do things we otherwise would never have done." She got into her car and jammed her keys in the ignition.

She believed that?

A big white truck pulled into the lot and parked in a spot near the beach.

"Dammit, there's the hospitality guys," Delaney said. "I knew they'd come early. I knew it. I have to go." She started the engine and put the car into Reverse and he jumped back so he wouldn't get run over. "See you later. I'll let you know how the wedding goes."

"Okay. And, Delaney…"

She'd already backed out. He watched her drive away, then climbed into his SUV. He replayed their night on the beach, thinking about the woman he'd made love to on a blanket in the sand. Fatigue? No way. This wasn't about fatigue at all.

DELANEY ARRIVED BACK at the beach at exactly eight o'clock and found the hospitality staff and the florist already hard at work. She jumped out of her car and smoothed her tan skirt, which she'd quickly ironed as soon as she got home. For all the turmoil of her morning so far, she'd still managed to stay on her original schedule. She hurried to the reception tent.

The tables had been set up, the white tablecloths spread. Against this ground the white calla lilies and purple orchids looked even more exotic. Delaney left the tent and went over to the rows of chairs that had been arranged facing the bay. Here, beneath the summer sky, the bride and groom would take their vows with the cobalt-blue of Green Bay as a backdrop. She slowly walked down the aisle, the chairs on either side adorned with the beautiful arrangements she and Karen had made yesterday. She stopped under the wedding arbor, decorated with orchids and callas and roses, and suddenly felt the tremulous anticipation of a bride.

Karen came over to her, smiling.

"It's even more beautiful than I imagined," Delaney said.

"You should be proud—you helped make this possible. Where would you like the bouquets, boutonnieres and corsages? They're still in the van."

"Just put them in my car. I'll run them over to the inn where the bridal party is getting dressed." She handed her keys to Karen and veered away toward a blue-jeaned man opening the back of a horse trailer.

"Everything ready to go?" she asked him.

"Yup. Takin' him down there right now. Rather have him in the fresh air than cooped up in here for the next couple hours." He backed a white horse out of the trailer, the same horse Delaney had watched the bride practice riding. In the confines of the trailer, the animal appeared even larger than he had in the corral.

"I'll be back thirty minutes before the ceremony starts," Delaney said. "Once the processional gets under way, I'll meet you to help the bride." She debated going down the beach with him to discuss tethering the horse farther around the bend. Then decided against it. She didn't want to return to the spot where she and Mike had made love last night. She didn't want to remember what he tasted like. Didn't want to remember what it felt like to have him on top of her. Didn't want to have to keep working at not feeling anything.

As the handler led the horse across the parking lot and onto the sand, she crossed her fingers that everything would come off without a hitch. After the processional, a duet would sing "The Wedding Song," trumpets would blare and the bride, wearing an elegant white gown, would come around the bend, riding sidesaddle on the white horse. Everything on cue. Just like in the movies. Too bad she wouldn't have the option of another take if it all went wrong.

She closed her eyes for a moment and prayed for the best. It would be one thing if the girl was an accomplished rider, but by her own admission, she had only been on a horse a couple of times—and then, only to learn sidesaddle for her wedding. This could turn out to be perfect…for the blooper reel.

She wandered to the edge of the water and watched the shallow waves breaking out on Green Bay. In the darkness last night, the water had almost seemed black—

No. She wasn't going to do this to herself. Those who failed to remember history were destined to repeat it. And she wasn't going to repeat what her mother had lived.

Thirty minutes later Delaney carried the box of flowers for the bridal party into the quaint inn where they were all dressing. The mother of the bride, Mrs. Farrell, accosted her almost the moment she stepped through the door. "Delaney! I'm so glad you're here. Laura doesn't like the garter."

Delaney fought to keep her eyes from rolling right up to the ceiling. She made her way to the guest room where the bride was ensconced. "You're absolutely beautiful, Laura. Now, what could be wrong on such a perfect day?" she said in a saccharine-sweet voice.

"My garter is too tight."

"Let me take a look."

Laura pulled up the hem of her dress to reveal the garter high on her thigh. Delaney almost choked on the laugh she was holding in.

Was there something about weddings that turned women into imbeciles? "The garter's only symbolic, hon," she said. "Since it's not holding up hosiery, just pull it down to your knee—even below if you want. It'll be a lot more comfortable."

Laura pulled the garter lower. "What would we do without you?"

"What indeed?" Delaney said in that same saccharine voice. Yes, she was getting good at this, if she did say so herself. She peeked through the slatted shutter in the window to spot two white limousines pulling into the lot. "The limos are here. It's almost time. Any last concerns or questions about anything? The ceremony? The horse? Anything?"

The bride shook her head.

"Okay, then. I need to pin the boutonnieres on the guys. See you at the beach." She hugged the bride. *Showtime,* she said to herself. This was going to be fun.

An hour later, Delaney had the bridal party lined up and ready to go. She was delighted at how beautiful everyone looked, the bridesmaids in tea-length pastel blue dresses, the groom and groomsmen in sand-colored linen suits with powder-blue dress shirts. As soon as the processional started, she took off through the woods to the beach where the horse was tethered. With any luck, the bride was already in the sidesaddle.

As she neared, she could see the handler holding the horse's reins and the bride standing several feet away. Uh-oh.

"What's going on?" she asked.

Neither said a word. Delaney glanced between the two. "Someone talk. Now."

"I don't think I can do it," the bride said, staring at the horse.

Delaney blew out a breath. For God's sake, she should have seen this coming last week when the girl was practically falling off the animal during riding practice. "You don't have to. No problem." The saccharine voice was coming to her easily now.

"You don't think everyone will be upset?"

"Not at all. They'll understand." She touched the handler on the arm. "Don't you agree?"

"I—I don't know…"

Delaney waved a hand. She had no time for equivocating. "That's because you have a vested interest. Believe me, everyone will get over it." From down the beach she could hear "The Wedding Song" begin. Time to get this bride to the aisle.

"That's a relief." Laura visibly relaxed. "I don't want Nick to be hurt."

Delaney put an arm around the girl's shoulders. "Honey, all Nick really cares about is that you become his wife."

Mrs. Farrell burst out of the trees, puffing. "What's going on?"

"Nothing!" Delaney, the handler and the bride said in unison.

Delaney stepped into Mrs. Farrell's path and the woman neatly sidestepped her and made a beeline for her daughter. "Everyone is waiting. You need to get on that horse and get going." She glared at Delaney. "We're behind schedule."

"I can't do it," Laura said.

"Do what?"

"Ride the horse," Delaney said at the same moment Laura said, "Get married."

Delaney stared at the bride, visions of her inheritance evaporating. "What?"

"I can't get married."

"I thought you couldn't ride the horse!"

"Why wouldn't I be able to ride the horse? I've been practicing. And it's so romantic." She ran a hand down the animal's neck. "I just can't get married."

"This is ridiculous!" Mrs. Farrell cried. "You get on that horse—"

"No."

"Honey, please." She faced Delaney. "You tell her. She'll listen to you. Everyone feels like this before they get married."

"Everyone feels like this before they get married," Delaney repeated.

"*I* didn't," the handler said.

"Be quiet," Delaney and Mrs. Farrell told him.

"Go ahead." Mrs. Farrell waved a hand at Delaney, her bracelets clattering.

She was supposed to convince the bride to buy into the myth?

And if she didn't, everyone's inheritance was as good as gone.

Delaney looked at the young woman and knew she couldn't lie. "Don't do it," she said softly. "Don't do it unless you're sure. Because the odds aren't with you. Every day lots of new marriages begin…and lots of old ones falter…and lots of them fail."

Mrs. Farrell's face flamed red, but Delaney ignored her.

"'They lived happily ever after' is a myth, a fairy tale put out there by Snow White and Cinderella and—"

"That's quite enough," Mrs. Farrell snapped.

"—Sleeping Beauty. They all got a prince, but what did they give up to get them? And who truly knows how things turned out in the long run?"

"You're fired," Mrs. Farrell said.

Well, no need to stop now, then. "So if you don't want to get married, don't. Go write your own life's story without this guy."

"Honey, don't listen to her, she's just—"

"Shut up, Mother." Tears welled up in Laura's eyes.

Delaney clenched her teeth. Did she really want to be responsible for this girl not getting married? She took hold of Laura's arms and dove into uncharted territory. "But if by some chance, some wonderful chance, you are one of the lucky ones who somehow found the man who is her other half, the man without whom the days just aren't complete and the nights are empty, you should get down on your knees in gratitude. And then you should marry him."

The maid of honor broke out of the woods, her expression frantic. "What is going on? They've done the song twice already and they're starting again."

"Take my mother back to the wedding," Laura said.

"But what's going on?" Laura's best friend took hold of Mrs. Farrell's arm.

"That's it? You want me to go out there and tell everyone it's off?" Mrs. Farrell put a hand to her forehead. "I need an aspirin."

"It's off?" The maid of honor stopped in her tracks.

Laura looked at Delaney for a very long moment. Then she said, "I can't even imagine my life without him."

Another hopeless romantic. Delaney was almost beginning to envy their foolish optimism.

The bride turned to the handler. "I'm ready. Let's go."

He helped her up onto the horse. She straightened her beaded white dress and smiled down at them. "Get to your places, everyone. I'm getting married today...and we're late."

"YOU WANT TO GO HIT some balls at the play-ground?" Dan stood on Mike's front stoop, baseball glove on his left hand and a cap backward on his head.

It felt like they were twelve-year-olds again.

"What about Megan and Kristian?"

"Kristian's napping. Megan's washing the

kitchen floor. Kicked me out of the house. Said she's nesting and I'm hovering and driving her nuts and she'll call if she goes into labor."

"Isn't washing the floor sort of dangerous with her so pregnant?"

"That's what I said. That's when she kicked me out." Dan stepped into the house.

"Yeah, I'll come." Mike turned and yelled down the hall. "Hey, Andy, you want to go hit balls at the playground?"

His daughter rounded the corner from the kitchen and gave him two thumbs-up. "Okay."

They grabbed their baseball gloves, a metal bat and some balls from the garage and headed down the sidewalk to the schoolyard a couple of blocks away.

"It's almost summer!" Andy sang, skipping ahead of them in shorts and running shoes. "Seven more days of school!" Half a block up, she spun and ran back to throw herself into Mike's arms and give him a hug. "I love you!"

"I love you, too." He laughed.

She fell into step beside him and clasped his hand. "So where were you last night?"

He blinked. She'd slept at a friend's house; how did she know he hadn't come home? "Home."

"Then how come when you picked me up this morning you had on the same clothes as yesterday?"

Dan cleared his throat.

"Because they were…handy. Right on the floor. And it's Saturday. And since when did you start caring what I wear, anyway?"

Andy shrugged and let go of his hand to run ahead of them down the sidewalk again.

"You're wearing the same clothes as yesterday?" Dan asked. "Sounds suspicious to me, too."

Mike threw him a warning look. "I'm showered and changed now."

"Hmm, seems to me there's a story in there somewhere," Dan muttered.

Andy raced back toward them. "Rock, paper, scissors to see who hits first!"

Five minutes later, they reached the schoolyard with all major decisions made: Mike was hitting, Dan was pitching, and Andy was covering the outfield. As she jogged to center field, Dan turned to Mike.

"So, what'd you do last night?"

"Helped Delaney." Mike tossed the extra balls toward the pitcher's mound.

"Delaney?" Dan drew her name out slowly. "You mean Pumpkin?"

"No. I mean Delaney."

"Ohh. I sense a shift of some sort. Let me think about this." Dan picked up the bat and took a couple of practice swings. "She doesn't have a job to go back to, so you no longer have to romance her to keep her in town. But you're spending time with her, anyway. What could this mean? Did someone hit a single last night?"

"It doesn't mean a thing," Mike lied.

"The hell it doesn't." Dan handed over the bat and headed out to the pitcher's mound. "That's okay," he said over his shoulder. "I've got the rest of the afternoon to get it out of you." He positioned himself in a pitcher's stance, then lobbed a ball toward Mike who let it fly past. It crashed into the backstop fence and rolled to a stop.

"Stee-rike," Dan called out.

"Ball one," Mike said. "That was so low, if I'd hit it, I'd be golfing."

"Let's see. You went to Chicago, came back to work, Delaney went to the florist's. So where'd you help her last night?" Dan called as he let loose the next pitch.

Mike hit a line drive up the first base side and Andy chased it deep into the outfield. "At the beach."

"The beach." Dan began to chortle. "Timing submarine races?"

"Setting up for the wedding."

Andy ran up to Dan and tossed him the ball underhand. He threw another pitch and Mike popped up to center field, sending Andy running again.

"What's to set up? That's for the rental company to do."

Mike shrugged as Dan came toward him. "Spill it. What were you doing at the beach?" Dan asked in a low voice even though Andy was on the other side of the field. *"Pumpkin?"*

"Don't be crude."

A shout from Andy drew their attention. She hefted the ball and it hit the ground twenty feet away.

Dan grinned. "Wow. I'm right. Pumpkin McBride. You were doing Pumpkin."

"If you open your mouth, or in any way let her know that you know, I will put you permanently in the trunk of that '57 Chevy."

Dan put both hands up in surrender. "You know me. No secrets ever escape these lips."

"I mean it. You open your mouth and I'll kill you."

"Okay, okay, okay. Don't worry. Hey, I'm glad for you."

"I don't know. She *is* leaving town in two months."

"So?"

"Hey, hit the ball!" Andy yelled from the outfield. "This is your last at bat! Then I'm up!"

"Keep your pants on!" Mike yelled back. He looked at Dan. "And I have Andy to consider." He walked back to home plate and swung at the next pitch, hitting a solid grounder into left field.

Dan jogged toward him. "Why would Andy have to know about it?"

"Are you kidding? Andy knows everything. She'd find out about this soon enough. I don't want her to get attached to Delaney and then hurt when she goes back to Boston." And she was going back—of that he was certain.

"Yeah, but isn't Andy working at the wedding shop almost every day after school?"

Mike shook his head. "Delaney's just her boss there. Not a woman her father's involved with."

"You're splitting hairs. Andy's already attached to her. She talks about Pumpkin… Delaney all the time."

"All the more reason for me not to get involved. I've thought it over. It's just not a good idea." Mike set the end of the bat on the ground, leaned on the handle and decided to change the subject. "Hey, but get this. Her uncle was at the florist's the day the thermostat got turned down and all the flowers froze."

"The conspiracy returns."

Dan's cell rang and he dug it out of his pocket and flipped it open. "Hi, hon." He paused. "Are you kidding? I'm on my way. Yeah. No. I'll be right there. Don't do anything." He paused. *"I won't get in an accident."* He shut off the phone and slapped Mike on the shoulder. "Guess what?"

"She's in labor."

Dan nodded. "Her water just broke. And her folks are down in Green Bay. Can you and Andy babysit Kristian until they get back? It'll be about an hour."

"No problem." Mike waved Andy in. "Hey, kid, Megan's going to have the baby. You want to babysit Kristian a while?"

Andy gave a whoop and charged toward them. And all three took off running for home.

CHAPTER TEN

As DUSK FELL, Mike wandered outside to sit in one of the director's chairs on his backyard deck. He'd always heard second babies came faster, but there wasn't a word from Dan and Megan yet. He considered stopping at the wedding to see Delaney, but couldn't think of a good reason for being there other than wanting to make sure everything went well. Seemed like a weak excuse, considering he wasn't the wedding planner.

He leaned back in the chair and closed his eyes. Maybe he would just sit here a while and think about…stuff. His marriage. His ex-wife. His daughter. His life. His goals and dreams. New babies. Love.

Delaney.

Naked and soft and hot.

His eyes popped open.

Andy charged out the back door with her friend Brittany. "Hey, Dad, can I go over to

Britty's and roast marshmallows and make s'mores? Did Dan call yet? Did Megan have a baby?"

"No baby yet, as far as I know. And, yeah, you can go to Britty's. I'm probably going over to the wedding for a while, make sure everything's going okay for Delaney. I won't be gone long. Call me on the cell before—"

"Okay, see you later." Andy and Britty raced around the side of the house toward the front yard.

"—you come home." It was nice to see her so happy. She hardly put up a fuss about doing her homework anymore, and he suspected working at the wedding shop with Delaney was the difference.

He studied the golden-hued sky and considered Delaney's conspiracy theory. Given the conversation Delaney overheard and the oddball things that had gone wrong with this wedding, not to mention that Lou Waverly had motive and he *had* been in the flower shop at just the right time…

They should monitor the next wedding more closely. Keep the names of the vendors close to the vest. Float some false vendor names as a diversion, then see if disaster struck any of them. Might put a spotlight on the guilty party—if there truly was one.

He should probably tell Delaney this. *Right away.* And besides, she'd surely want to know that Megan was in labor.

DELANEY WATCHED THE wedding party from the edge of the portable dance floor. The couple was married. The horse hadn't thrown the bride. The mother had recanted and rehired Delaney. All was right with the world.

Well, at least with the world of weddings. Her personal life, now that was another story.

She felt a hand on her arm and turned. *Mike.* Her stomach flip-flopped. "What are you doing here?"

"Megan went into labor."

"She did?"

He nodded. "They're at the hospital. Megan's parents are watching Kristian. And Andy's gone to a friend's house…"

"So you came to the wedding of someone you don't even know?" she teased.

"After everything we've been through the past few days, I kind of feel like I know them."

"Apparently not well enough. The bride almost changed her mind at the last minute."

She read the surprise in his blue eyes and grinned.

"What happened?" he asked.

"I convinced her that happy endings were possible."

Mike looked up at the sky and Delaney followed his gaze. "What are you doing?" she asked.

"Getting ready for a lightning bolt," he said.

"Very funny. She believed me and that's all that matters. So Megan's in the hospital?" For a moment she wondered what it would be like to have a baby, a child to raise, to love. And a husband to share all that with.

The band began to play a slow song, soft and romantic, and couples paired off on the dance floor. An unfamiliar ache squeezed her heart. Babies, husbands, romance. Good God, what was the matter with her these days?

"Yeah. Dan said he'd call as soon as there was any news."

They stood side by side for several minutes, watching the dancers without saying a word.

"Want to dance?" Mike asked.

Them? Here? Now? She shook her head.

"Come on. A celebration dance. You succeeded against the odds once again."

"I...have to work." The music floated over her. *No.* For him, maybe, it was a celebration dance. For her, it was a reminder that she'd made another stupid decision where a man was concerned.

"No one needs you right now. Come on." He took her hand and gave it a gentle tug. She resisted only a second before following him down the beach to the spot where they'd made love the night before. As the music carried toward them on the soft night breeze and the moon reflected in the bay, he took her in his arms and they began to dance. Mike drew her closer and tucked her head against his chest. She shivered, a delicious shiver of anticipation, and gave in to the rush of feelings she'd been trying to keep at bay.

She thought to herself that maybe her mother had done it all wrong, maybe it had been her mother's own fault that nothing worked out for her, maybe Delaney and Mike had been fated to be together and now all the pieces had come together at just the right time to make this work. She looked up at him, at those eyes, and for the briefest moment was tempted to bare her soul.

"I have an idea," Mike said softly.

That we should make love in the sand

again? Delaney's heart sped up and she pulled back to look at him.

HE TOOK IN HER wide hazel eyes and the natural blush across her cheekbones...and thought of her under him, naked, her red hair tousled like Medusa.

"I have an idea about the conspiracy theory," he said, trying to keep his voice steady. "If you're right, if someone is in fact trying to keep you from succeeding—"

"Someone, meaning my uncle?"

He shrugged. "I struggle to believe he's behind anything."

"Me, too. But right now, he's the only person with motive. Maybe we should just confront him."

Mike wanted to run his fingers through that red hair, tip her head back and kiss her hard for making such an innocent suggestion. "Delaney, nice thought, but no. You can't just go around accusing people of crimes. First of all, no one would ever admit they were responsible. The florist lost thousands of dollars' worth of flowers. There'd be restitution to make, not to mention legal charges."

"You're right. Sometimes I don't know

where my head's at. Besides, I'd hate to make an accusation and be wrong."

"That's why I think we should try to flush the culprit out," Mike said. "If there is a culprit."

"How?"

"Plant some false information. Hell, feed it directly to him and anyone else we can think of who might have motive, then wait and watch."

"You mean like tell him the name of a different baker than we're actually going to use? And if that baker's oven explodes we know it's him?"

"Something like that."

The song ended and they pulled apart.

Delaney nodded. "I like that we'll be proactive. I've been working too hard to hold these weddings together. As unimaginative as your idea sounds—"

"Unimaginative?" He put a hand over his heart as though mortally wounded.

"Unimaginative, stereotypical, theatrical." She smiled. "But if my uncle or someone else is behind my troubles, I want to expose them."

"Good. We'll have to figure out a plan."

They headed back toward the reception tent and Delaney's arm brushed his. "About last night," he said slowly. "I didn't come down to the beach expecting…"

"Sometimes these things happen," she said briskly. "Circumstances. Happenstance. Doesn't mean anything. Certainly nothing with long-term ramifications."

"No. Certainly not." It sounded like Delaney had performed a business analysis of the situation and decided against the investment. Which was the same conclusion he'd come to himself this afternoon, even if she did keep jumping naked into his mind. "We should just put it behind us."

"Yes."

"Pretend it never happened. Go back to being friends."

"Absolutely."

He looked at her, but she kept her eyes straight ahead. Damn, she was beautiful. "Before we do that, though, I need to make one thing clear. It wasn't fatigue."

That got her. She turned. "What?"

"It wasn't the fatigue and it wasn't the beer and it wasn't the moon and the waves."

She stared at him a long moment, then shrugged. "Believe what you want," she said in a brittle voice. "I know better."

Mike's cell phone vibrated in his back

pocket and he pulled it out to check the caller ID. "It's Dan. You know what that means." He flipped open the phone. "Is it safe to say congratulations, yet?"

DELANEY WALKED WITH MIKE down the mauve-striped hallway of the hospital maternity ward early the next afternoon. A baby boy. Megan and Dan had another son. They stopped at the long viewing window to peek in at the newborns swaddled in their bassinets. Delaney shifted the gift bag to her other hand. "I don't see a crib card for Hobart."

"The baby's in their room," someone said and Delaney turned to see Dan's parents just a few feet away.

"We're going down to the cafeteria to get a cup of coffee," his mom said.

"How's the baby?" Mike asked.

"He's a sweetheart. Go on in, they'll be thrilled to see you. Fourth door on the right." She pointed down the hall. "Dan's sisters sent the most gorgeous flowers. Wait'll you see them."

The door to Megan's room was ajar and Mike tapped lightly before pushing it open and stepping inside. Delaney paused in the doorway. Soft afternoon light filtered through the window and cast a warm glow on Dan in the rocking chair, the new baby in his arms. Megan stood beside him in a pale pink robe, head bent next to his as they watched their child sleep. Delaney caught her breath.

"Hey, guys," Mike said quietly. "Congratulations."

Delaney handed their gift to Megan and gave her a hug. "He's beautiful."

"Hey, Sebastian," Mike said. "Looks just like his brother."

"Yeah. We're hoping he has less energy than Kristian," Dan said.

Mike laughed. "Hate to tell you, but Kristian will teach him everything he knows, so it's a lost cause anyway. It's what siblings do."

Delaney joined him on the edge of the bed.

"So little Seabass arrived at eight-thirty last night, huh?" Mike said.

"Eight-thirty-three. It went fast compared to the first one. Thanks for watching Kristian until my folks got back." Megan lowered herself into the overstuffed easy chair in the corner. She looked at Delaney. "How'd the wedding go yesterday?"

"Great," Delaney answered.

"The bride almost pulled out, but it came off without a hitch," Mike added.

Dan lifted his gaze from the new baby and planted it firmly on Mike. "You were there, too?"

"He wanted to talk about setting up a sting to catch the saboteur before the next wedding," Delaney said quickly.

"You mean you've bought into the conspiracy theory now?" Dan asked Mike.

"Well, uh, no…yeah…I don't know. I'm not convinced it's Lou Waverly. We're just going to try something, see if we can flush anyone out," Mike said.

Dan laughed out loud.

"We put out some false information," Delaney said. "Like…we say we're using a different bakery than we're actually using. Then, if something goes wrong there, we can be reasonably sure there's a culprit."

Dan snorted. "What? Are you two writing movie scripts now?"

The baby stirred and opened his eyes a crack and all four adults froze. Sebastian promptly fell back to sleep.

"I think it's brilliant," Megan said.

"How will this catch the thief, so to speak?" Dan asked. "Let's say the baker's oven quits working. There's no proof a person, let alone Lou Waverly, is responsible."

"Got a better idea?" Mike crossed his arms over his chest.

"We've had three suspicious incidents already. Why wait for six before we take action? If we're wrong, then all we've wasted is some talk," Delaney said.

The baby stirred again and Megan took him from Dan and nuzzled her cheek against his forehead. Then she gently laid him in Mike's arms. He smiled at the baby. "Hey there, Sebastian, glad you finally made it." He brushed his thumb against the baby's cheek and cradled him close to his body. Sebastian let out a tiny sigh and settled back to sleep.

Delaney envied the ease with which Mike held the child, and suddenly she wished it were their child he was holding.

"The baby had to be footprinted for his birth certificate." Megan sipped at the straw in her disposable cup. "Then, they had to get the ink off so his foot wasn't stained."

All three looked at her.

"It doesn't hurt him, hon," Dan said.

Megan rolled her eyes. "I'm thinking about the ink. On cop shows, they put this invisible powder on, like, the doorknobs or the lock to the safe. And when the criminal tries to break in, the powder stains their hands and it won't wash off."

"Sebastian," Mike said to the baby, "I think your mama wants to be a private detective. She's worse than I am."

"Think about it. How better to ID the perp?" Megan said.

"ID the perp?" Dan echoed incredulously.

"Maybe she's onto something." Delaney gestured toward Mike and Dan. "You guys know a cop?"

"We all know cops," Dan said. "It's a small town. But if we ask about something as dumb as this, we're going to have to spill what we're up to and—"

"Where the hell would we use it, anyway? It's not like we're protecting a treasure that's locked up," Mike said.

The baby squawked and Mike threw a panicked look at Megan.

"He's getting hungry." She nodded at Delaney. "You want to hold him before he wakes up?"

"I…uh…" Oh, God, she wasn't even sure she knew how. What if she let his neck fall backward? Or touched that soft spot on the top of his head? She had no experience with babies. Before she could formulate an excuse, Mike had gently placed Sebastian in her arms. She held the baby gingerly, as she'd held every baby that had been thrust at her over the years.

"Couldn't we just put that powder on the thermostat at the florist and see if someone ends up with colorful fingers?" Megan said.

Dan shook his head. "Only an idiot would do the same thing twice."

"Never say never," Delaney said.

"Lame. Really lame," Dan insisted.

"Okay, spymasters," Mike said, ignoring him. "Assume we figure out where to put this stuff so it can end up on the bad guy's fingers. Where are we going to get it?"

"Easy." Megan grinned. "The Internet."

"You three are beginning to scare me." Dan looked at his wife. "And, Megan, where did you learn this stuff?"

A nurse stepped into the room and all four shut up. *Like guilty teenagers planning to sneak out of the house at midnight,* Delaney thought.

"I need to check your vitals, but I can come back," the nurse said to Megan.

"Knock, knock," another woman said from the door.

Lou, Claire and a stuffed black bear came

through the door just as the nurse left. "We heard at church this morning that the little one arrived," Lou said. "And we had this gift all ready."

"It's faux mink," Claire added.

Lou bent toward the child and Delaney felt a surge of protectiveness. She held Sebastian closer.

"He's beautiful," Claire said.

While Lou and Claire chatted with the others, Delaney touched the downy hair on Sebastian's head and inhaled the sweet smells of lotion and powder. The baby opened his eyes and stared up at her, then pursed his lips, making a squeak before falling back to sleep. She cradled him close and touched her lips to the butter-soft skin of his forehead.

"Delaney? Are you listening?" Mike asked.

She looked up. "Did I miss something?"

Everyone laughed.

"Babies do that to you," Megan said.

Delaney smiled. "Sorry."

"Don't forget to check with the manager of the Dalton House about the sprinkler system," Megan said.

Delaney squinted at her. The Dalton House, a 1920s Tudor Revival manor with beautifully landscaped grounds, was the site of the next wedding. Why would Megan bring this up now? She glanced at Lou and Claire. Unless… "Okay."

"Where the wedding is this weekend," Megan said. "I heard they've actually forgotten to change the timer on the sprinklers before an event and the system has gone off at the worst times." Megan waved a hand. "Drenching the guests."

"I've never heard of such a thing," Claire said.

Megan nodded. "It's true. Dan used to mow the lawn there in high school and it happened, didn't it, Dan?"

"A couple of times."

"You sure don't want that on Saturday," Megan said.

"Yeah. Imagine the entire wedding party looking like they're in a wet T-shirt contest," Dan said. "Come to think of it, maybe you should let the sprinklers go off."

"Daniel," Megan warned.

"I'll talk to the groundskeeper," Delaney said.

"Maybe you should check the timer yourself just to be safe," Mike said. "Do you know anything about setting one?"

She shook her head. "But how hard can it be? All I need to find is the on/off switch." Sebastian's eyes opened again and then closed. "Megan, he's really starting to wake up."

Megan slid out of her chair. "It's been three hours since he ate."

"You're probably better off letting the management fool with the timer," Lou said. "So nothing gets out of whack."

Delaney shrugged. "Maybe. Just in case, though... Do you know where the timer is, Dan? In an outbuilding somewhere?"

"No. It's on the outside wall of the carriage house. Gray box. You can't miss it."

"I'd think it would be locked," Lou said.

"Not usually," Dan said. "At least not back when I worked there."

Sebastian shifted and yawned, killing the conversation. He squirmed in Delaney's arms, eyes open, and let out another squawk. She couldn't believe how sweet he was.

"It's time. This boy needs to eat." Megan took Sebastian and began to rock him in her arms.

"We'll be on our way, then," Claire said.

"Congratulations to you both," Lou added.

As soon as they were gone, Delaney shut the door firmly. "I know that was a setup. But was it true? Have the sprinklers gone off during events?"

Megan let out a short laugh. "No. That was the best I could come up with on the spur of the moment."

"It was a good lie," Mike said. "I was impressed."

Megan smiled proudly. "I think Lou and Claire bought it. Now you guys take over and flush Lou out."

"How?" Delaney asked.

"Detection powder." Megan laughed. "Get on the ball, Delaney. Put it on the timer, then watch the color of your uncle's fingers."

"I don't know about this. Anyone could touch the timer—not just Lou. And then where would we be?" Mike said. "I think detection powder should be a last-resort thing."

"You think?" Dan said.

"Hey, it's a good—" Megan began, but stopped when Sebastian began to fuss in earnest.

"We'll get out of here, too." Mike started for the door.

Delaney followed him out, stopping in the doorway to look back at Dan and Megan. "Congratulations. He's a beautiful baby." A lump rose in her throat and she swallowed it down. For the first time in as long as she could remember, she was truly envious of a relationship.

CHAPTER ELEVEN

THE BELLS JANGLED as the door banged against the opposite wall. "Ms. McBride!" someone called from the front of the store.

Delaney finished writing "masking tape" on her shopping list. "Back here!" was all she got out before the owner of Eleganza Cucina, the caterer for the upcoming wedding, sashayed into the back room.

"I have terrible news. Terrible. They shut me down," she said, a slight Italian accent evident in her voice.

"Shut what down?"

"My business."

Delaney felt the stirrings of panic. Not another disaster. "Hold on, Annalisa. What are you talking about?"

"A visitor came today from the Department of Health. A surprise inspection. They got an anonymous call. And they shut me down."

"How can they shut you down? You have a wedding to cater this weekend."

"I told him that. He said I had an unlicensed facility."

"Do you?" Delaney couldn't believe this was happening.

"Well, no, I didn't think so. But, yes, I guess I do. I cook out of my home."

Delaney didn't even want to ask the next question because she dreaded the answer. "Can you get your home licensed before Saturday?"

"Oh my, no. He said in order for me to do that—" Annalisa composed herself "—I would have to get commercial ovens and refrigerators, a fire-prevention system, take safety and management courses—"

"That's enough." Delaney held up a hand. The muscles at the back of her neck felt like steel cords. "How could you not have known this?" Anger and frustration were showing in her voice and she didn't care.

"I'm new to catering."

"You've never done this before?"

"Not cooking. *Catering.*" She splayed a hand across on her chest. "I am a *chef.* I cook at other people's homes. The bride's parents have hired me many times before. So when they asked, could I do the wedding, I never even thought about licensing."

Delaney squeezed the back of her neck. "Let me get this straight. If this wedding was in someone's house and you cooked in their kitchen, it would be okay."

"Yes."

"But because you're going to cook at home and move the food somewhere else, your kitchen has to be licensed?"

Annalisa nodded.

"This may sound overly simplistic, but can't you just cook everything at the reception site?"

"The Dalton House?" Annalisa shook her head. "They quit building it during the depression. When they finally finished it, they turned it into a museum. It only has a sink, warming ovens and a refrigerator. It's for staging the food, not cooking."

Delaney sighed. "What would happen if you did it, anyway?"

"He said if I didn't 'cease operations immediately,' they'd bring me in front of a judge. He gave me a verbal warning to shut down and said a follow-up letter would come in the mail."

Delaney stood and paced across the room. "So where does this leave us?"

"I need a licensed kitchen to cook in—or you have to find another caterer."

"This is one of the busiest wedding weekends of the year. It's June, for God's sake. The best caterers are booked a year out." She exhaled sharply. "Do you know anyone with a licensed kitchen you can use?"

Annalisa shook her head again. "Other caterers will need their kitchens Saturday. Like you say, it's the big wedding month. Restaurants—they need their kitchens, too, to feed their customers. Maybe a school or a church. But it's such short notice. I can make some calls…"

That was pretty much the answer she expected. "Okay. You think on this. I'll think on it, too. There's got to be an answer."

As soon as the door closed behind Annalisa, Delaney slammed her hand against the desk. There was no longer any doubt in her mind that someone was behind this. And her uncle was the most likely culprit. She'd probably never be able to find a licensed kitchen for this weekend. And as for finding another caterer, well… The bride was having a turn-of-the-century formal garden reception with a very unusual menu. Delaney might be able to find someone willing to cook but it wouldn't be what the bride ordered. Or if it was, no way would it be made correctly.

Goodbye, inheritance.

She picked up the phone and called Mike at his law office. "The wedding saboteur has struck again. The Department of Health just shut down the caterer for this Saturday's wedding." She explained the whole story. "*Someone* knew her home wasn't licensed."

"That greedy son of a bitch," Mike said.

"Glad to know we're on the same page."

"Why don't you call the inspector and see if he got a name?"

Delaney tapped a finger on her desk. "He told Annalisa he got an anonymous phone call. So whoever it was made sure they were covering their tracks."

By the time they finished the call, Mike had become a true conspiracy-theory believer and Delaney had become so dejected she wanted to cry. For the next twenty minutes, she sat at her desk and did absolutely nothing. If her uncle wanted the money so badly, let him have it.

The thought triggered a rebellion in her brain. No way. She wasn't going down without a fight.

Reaching in the drawer, she pulled out the telephone book and her aunt's catering file and began to make calls. Over the course of the next two hours, she learned that none of the church or school kitchens were an option—either they were already being used or had a policy against renting out their kitchens. As for caterers, she found just one available. Delaney looked at the business card again—"Millie's Marvelous Meals."

How could she possibly go wrong with a caterer called that?

Swallowing hard, she called Millie back and detailed the situation. "As I mentioned in the first call, the ingredients have all been ordered. They just need to be prepared," she said.

Millie squeaked out a laugh. "I've never made lobster-stuffed filet mignon before. I usually do simpler meals. But I'm willing to try." She managed to sound apologetic and hopeful at the same time.

I'll try. Delaney could see the big red F on the evaluation form.

"I'll go on the Internet and see what I can find out about making those dishes before this weekend," Millie added.

Wonderful. Now she felt so much better. Delaney could only imagine what would happen to the eggplant rollatini; the grilled new potatoes with baby onions; the mushrooms stuffed with escargot, goat cheese and caramelized onions.

She mentally slapped herself. At least she'd found a cook. And at least this woman was going to *try* to learn how to prepare the food correctly. Maybe Annalisa could assist with the preparation, or even better...

"It just occurred to me," she said. "Since you've never made these dishes before and time is so tight... Well, how would you feel about renting your kitchen to Annalisa for the day?"

There was a long pause. "My kitchen?"

"Yes."

"I am the chef in my kitchen."

"I understand, but I just thought that maybe it might make everything simpler all around."

The silence that greeted her last sentence dragged on so long Delaney thought Millie had hung up. "Uh, Millie?"

"I don't rent out my kitchen. I don't know any chefs who do. If you want *me* to prepare this meal, I would be glad to. I'll do my best to make it memorable."

"I'm sure it will be." Of that she had no doubt.

She might as well go for broke. "What about the possibility of Annalisa assisting you with the preparation? If this wedding dinner is successful, it could be a real boon to business for both of you. But a failure… Well, you know how word gets around."

"I see what you mean. I don't usually share my kitchen, but this is an unusual situation. It probably would be helpful to have Annalisa here, the two of us working together. We could even split payment for the job."

"I'm sure that would be fine with Annalisa."

"Then that's what we'll do. Why don't you have her give me a call?"

Delaney hung up and rubbed the back of her neck. Another crisis averted. This wedding planning was going to do her in, in ways the advertising world never have thought of. She walked out into the shop and picked up her mail from the slot by the door. Bills and more bills, forwarded from the post office in Boston.

Passing the shelves of white accessories, she picked up the tiara and veil Megan had plopped on her head the day she'd arrived just a couple of weeks ago. She'd known it would be hard when she got here; she just hadn't realized how hard. Tears pricked at the back of her eyes.

She wanted to see Mike, wanted him to put his arms around her and kiss her and take her back to the place they'd found on the beach that night where problems just didn't seem to exist. At least not until the sun came up.

Just another daydream that couldn't possibly happen. She got her shopping list from the desk and stuck a note on the door saying she'd gone to the hardware store and would be back soon. As she stepped over the threshold, she gave the doorknob a quick tug. The door slammed shut behind her and the bell jangled wildly. She grinned, her mood lifting.

She strode down the sidewalk, the sun overhead further brightening her disposition and hardening her determination. After a few minutes, she reached the old lannonstone building that housed True Value Hardware. She *would* get this inheritance. They all would. The more her uncle—or whoever—worked against her, the harder she would work to make sure it was he who failed and not her.

MIKE GRABBED DELANEY by the arm and pulled her down the aisle into plumbing supplies. Surprise flitted across her face. This was going to be fun. "I got it," he whispered.

She looked at him in confusion. "Got what? And what are you doing here?"

"Hunting for you."

"No privacy in this town," she said without animosity.

"You left a note on your door."

"Oh, yeah. So what'd you get? The flu?"

He leaned close to her ear. "Detection powder. Violet. I ordered it."

"You mean the stuff Megan was talking about?"

He nodded, feeling a little like the kid who'd just discovered where the Christmas candy was stashed.

"You've got to be kidding me! I thought you wanted to save it as a last resort."

"I think the caterer being shut down constitutes last resort. I called SpyWizard.com as soon as I got off the phone with you. I got a brush, too. Everything will be here tomorrow—overnight delivery. We just have to dust the sprinkler timer then wait for your uncle to touch it. If he's behind the problems you've been having, we'll know it."

"Will he be able to wash it off?" Delaney asked.

Mike shook his head. "His fingers will be stained purple for days. Nothing takes it off—not water, not acetone, not alcohol. He'll have no way to lie his way out of it."

"And you don't think just confronting him might get us the same information without having to go through all this?"

Mike rolled his eyes.

"Just thought I'd ask. But won't he notice purple powder on the timer?"

"It's silver gray when you put it on—the same color as the timer box. It only turns purple when it mixes with the natural oil of skin." Mike started to laugh. "The guy said that if the person tries to wash it off with water, the stain actually spreads."

A customer stopped to examine a nearby showerhead and Mike took Delaney's hand and tugged her into the next aisle. He regretted not taking her concerns about her uncle more seriously when she first voiced them. "By the way, Dan's on board, too. I told him about the caterer and he agrees, too many coincidences."

"What if Uncle Lou didn't fall for Megan's story?" Delaney asked. "It did sound a bit far-fetched. Besides, he could find out if it's true just by asking the grounds manager."

Mike put a hand on her shoulder and leaned close to her ear. Tried not to let the smell of her shampoo distract him. "He's not going to check it out. Because he can't risk anyone remembering that he was asking questions about the sprinkler system going off during events and then connecting him to the problem later."

"But there'll never be a problem, because we'll make absolutely sure the sprinklers are shut off."

"He doesn't know that."

Delaney frowned.

"What's the matter? I would think you, of all people, would be excited to do this."

She glanced up at him. "What if someone else has to legitimately change the timer and gets purple fingers and wipes the thing off?"

He couldn't believe she was balking. "First, even if that happens, their fingers probably won't turn purple right away. So they won't know where it came from. And second…"

She stepped out from under his hand and raised her eyebrows. "Second?"

He wanted to kiss the doubt off her face. "Second, what have we got to lose?"

She looked up at the ceiling and shook her head. "We've got nothing to lose. You're right. I'm in."

"Great. What are you doing tomorrow night?"

"I thought I'd wash my hair."

"Can it. We've got a mission."

THE PHONE RANG EARLY the next morning and woke Delaney from a sound sleep. Why, on the one day she decided to sleep in, after a stressful day solving problems in the wonderful, wacky world of weddings, did her phone have to ring at the crack of dawn?

She fumbled about on the nightstand until her fingers closed over her cell phone. Though the ID showed a Boston area code, she was too foggy to figure out what it meant. She flipped open the phone. "Hello?" she croaked.

"Delaney! Good morning," a vaguely familiar male voice said.

She lay back into her pillow, closed her eyes and struggled to place the voice. "Uh… good morning." This better not be a very jolly groom calling about some very stupid detail at seven-thirty in the morning.

"This is Ned Wagner. I hope I'm not calling too early."

Ned Wagner. Vice president at the agency? Her heart began to pound. She bolted upright and tried to force her mind to function. Holding the phone away from her head for a second, she cleared her throat as quietly as possible. "No. No. I've been up for a while."

"Super. Because I've got a proposition for you."

She grabbed a pencil and pad of paper from the nightstand drawer. "What's up?"

She'd never gotten a call at home from the VP before. And she rarely heard from him in the office, either. This was not a man who typically mingled in the trenches. His time was spent reeling in the big clients and then keeping them happy.

"Don't know if you've heard, but Avalon Cosmetics is having second thoughts about the ad agency they left us for."

"I did hear something about that. Didn't know if it was true or not."

"It's true. So true, they want to come back."

"Cool!" *Cool?* Couldn't she think of something more professional to say than *cool?* How about, *That's wonderful news.* Or, *How exciting.* Or even, *That's thrilling.*

"We're all pretty excited about it," he said.

There was that *excited* word.

"Thrilled actually," he continued.

And the *thrilled* word. She studied a crack running the length of the ceiling.

"We've had a couple of meetings with

them. Yesterday we learned they want us to be the agency of record again."

"That's *wonderful* news," she said in her best professional voice. Did it mean something for her? Why was he calling?

"They said we had the best group of people they'd ever worked with. And—"

Her heart was pounding so hard she could hear it in her ears. He couldn't possibly be about to say what she thought he was about to say.

"—they want their entire team back. We need you, Delaney. Are you available? Interested?"

She opened her mouth wide and punched the air with her left hand. Interested? She was ready to do cartwheels. "I've taken another position, actually." She tried to keep from sounding totally and completely ecstatic.

"We want you back," Ned said. "And we'll raise your salary ten percent to make your decision easier."

Holy cow, she'd won the lottery!

"So are you in? Can we tell Avalon you'll be back?"

"Yes. Tell them I can't wait to get started."

She threw off her covers and jumped out of bed to push aside the curtains. June sunshine and a warm breeze streamed through her open window. This was all she wanted. This and…

"We'd like to have a meeting with the whole team to get everyone up to speed. Can you be here Friday afternoon?"

This Friday? "You mean in three days?" She paced the room, working schedules in her head. She could fly into Boston Thursday night, meet with them Friday morning, then fly back out here Friday afternoon in time for the rehearsal dinner. It would be a stretch, but doable. With only two weddings left after this weekend, she could go back to Boston in a few weeks, back to her life, back to her job, back to a higher salary—all with one hundred thousand dollars in the bank. "Friday should be fine. I just have to check my schedule, but I don't think I have anything so important I can't move it." *Liar, liar, pants on fire.*

"Good, we fly out Saturday for Tokyo."

"Tokyo?" Surely they weren't going to the Avalon headquarters already. They had no advertising concepts to present yet.

"Sorry about the short notice. We're meeting at Avalon on Monday. It's more complicated than I've told you so far." Ned cleared his throat. "Their top management has concerns about marketing direction because they're firing the new agency after such a short time and they've got a new line of cosmetics they want to bring to market. So they've asked to have this initial meeting in their offices. The marketing director thinks it will settle everyone down."

"We get to roll out a new line?"

"Yeah. Package design, direct mail, TV, print, radio… You name it, we'll be doing it."

This was more than a dream come true, it was a miracle. Delaney danced a circle in the middle of her room.

"That's why we want you back on Friday—we need to strategize before we go."

Reality crashed the party in her brain. She could be there for the meeting Friday, but she couldn't be gone this weekend, not with the wedding. Her mind raced for a way to resolve the conflict. She dropped onto the edge of the bed and tried to still the racing of her heart. "Um, Toyko may be a problem." She cringed.

"I know this is short notice. But they're the client. They say jump and we ask how high." Ned chuckled.

How well she knew that. Delaney put a hand to her forehead. This wasn't how things were supposed to happen.

"We need you there, Delaney. We need the account executive there so the execs give their blessing to this changeover," Ned said with sudden intensity. "It's not one hundred percent yet. Close, but not there. We can't risk anything going wrong."

How could she say no? How could she turn down the job she so desperately needed?

But how could she desert Mike and the others?

"Delaney?"

"Yes?"

"If there's something you need to finish up before you come back, we can get by without you on Friday. But you have to be on that plane with us Saturday."

"Okay. I'll be there. Friday, Saturday, whenever you need me." Her stomach started to churn.

BY EARLY AFTERNOON, Delaney was a mess. She'd spent hours second-guessing her decision and trying to find some way to do everything, to make everyone happy, to keep the job and still finish the weddings. She couldn't concentrate, could barely think, and the phone kept ringing with one wedding-related call after another. Finally she grabbed her sunglasses, shoved some money in the pocket of her capris and took off with no specific destination in mind.

Swinging into the coffee shop, she grabbed an iced latte and headed to the park to work out the conflicts knotting up her brain. She passed the pond with its mother ducks and broods of ducklings, and envied the simplicity of their lives. Fly, swim, eat, lay eggs, raise babies.

Hide from hunters.

Okay, so maybe life wasn't so easy for them, either.

She took in a deep breath of summer— warm, clean air, blooming flowers, new-mown grass.

What should she do?

How could she tell Mike and the others she was leaving, that because of her, none of them would get their inheritance?

How could she stay here when the job she desperately needed to get out of debt had just been offered to her?

What if she didn't go to Tokyo and the agency lost their chance to get the account because she hadn't come along?

What if the agency offered the job to someone else?

What if she stayed for the wedding planning

and the Henrys didn't finish their part and she didn't get her inheritance, anyway? And then she had no job and no money?

She squeezed her eyes shut.

What about whatever was going on between Mike and her?

There was nothing going on between Mike and her.

Her brain felt like a spinning top.

She wandered across the park to where the new band shell was to be constructed. As she drew near, it became obvious that, while the demolition of the old structure was finished, rebuilding had yet to begin. A construction trailer was parked on-site, ready for the next phase, while a bulldozer loaded debris into a dump truck. She stopped to study a large sign showing an architectural rendition of the finished band shell.

"Pretty snazzy, huh?" someone said over her shoulder.

"The new one will be bigger than the old one, with much better sound," another man said.

She turned. "Hey, Stonewall, Sully. So you're ready to start construction?"

Sully rocked back on his heels. "Just about," he said.

"Finally." Stonewall tugged at one of his

long white eyebrows. "It took forever to get the city workers out here to tear the old one down."

"It didn't take *that* long," Sully said.

Delaney wanted to scream. She had no patience today for the bickering of these two.

"The old band shell was falling apart," Stonewall said. "Decayed wood, holes in the stage decking. It's been unsafe for years."

Delaney looked at Sully and waited for his counterargument.

"He's right about that," Sully said. "The city just didn't have any money to build a new one."

Her mouth dropped open.

"Thank goodness for Ellie," Stonewall said.

"Yes, where would we be without Ellie?" Sully agreed.

Delaney knew she was gaping. These guys may have just had a breakthrough of sorts. She should tell Mike.

"So what brings you out here today?" Sully asked. "Want to check our progress? Hoping for a tour?"

"Of our demolished band shell?" Stonewall muttered.

She debated how to answer. "Just going for a walk. I've got some things I need to figure out."

"Wedding stuff?" Stonewall pulled off his

baseball cap and wiped the sweat off his forehead.

Delaney shook her head. "Life stuff."

"We can help you with that," Sully said. "We've done our share of living."

"That's okay. But thanks, anyway."

"No, really. We have this method for making decisions," Stonewall said. "Henry Clark came up with it years ago."

Sully nodded.

These two were getting along way too well. "By any chance, does this decision-making method involve a bottle of Jameson?"

The two men exchanged a look. "How did you know?" Sully asked.

"Finest Irish whiskey there is," Delaney said, grinning.

Stonewall grinned back at her. "We just had some ourselves at lunch."

She never would have guessed.

"Okay, so what's this method you guys are talking about? I'm desperate."

"Well, we call it the three-step doctor's method," Stonewall said.

"Was one of you a doctor?"

"No." Stonewall stuck his hands in the pockets of his baggy jeans. "But Henry Clark was smart enough to have been one."

"I see," she said even though she didn't.

"It works like this," Sully said. "Step one, you list the pros. Step two, you list the cons. Step three, you do no harm."

"Do no harm?"

"If anything, either pro or con, will cause harm to someone else, that option is eliminated."

Delaney cocked her head, impressed. "First do no harm. The doctor's creed. How'd you guys come up with this?"

Sully snorted. "Stonewall had his heels dug in one night—"

"Now just wait one minute," Stonewall said.

"Fine. He and I couldn't agree one night," Sully said.

"You two? I can't believe it."

"And Henry Clark, fine man that he is, pulled out the Jameson," Sully said with an Irish brogue. "And after a wee bit o' Jameson—"

"Many wee bits o' Jameson," Stonewall interjected.

"Many wee bits o' Jameson," Sully agreed, "we'd figured it all out."

"I've got to get a bottle," Delaney said. She examined the artist's rendition again. "So you going to have this thing built by the Fourth?"

"Without a doubt," Sully said at the same moment Stonewall said, "When pigs fly."

Delaney laughed. "Thanks for your help, guys. I'd better get back to wedding planning and leave you to your work." She headed across the park thinking about the Henrys' decision-making process. "Probably works great for black-and-white issues," she murmured to herself. "But what happens when every option you have has the potential to harm someone else? Then what do you do?"

CHAPTER TWELVE

THE REST OF THE DAY went by in a haze as
Delaney agonized over whether she should
call the ad agency and turn down the job. Pro
by pro, con by con, she debated the arguments, finding each one strong in its own
right. By eight o'clock, when Mike picked
her up to sneak onto the grounds of the
Dalton House and put detection powder on
the timer, she was still vacillating.

Mike pulled into a parking space outside the
Tudor mansion and shut off the engine. "I
scoped it out already. Dan was right—the
timer's on the outside wall of the carriage
house, right next to the gas and electric meters."

Delaney studied the imposing stone
building. "Are you sure we're not doing this too
soon? It's only Tuesday. My uncle probably
won't try to mess with it until Friday." The day
she was supposed to be back in Boston.

Mike's eyes met hers. "I've got a game

tomorrow night. Thursday and Friday night they have big functions here. Way too many people will be around. We'd never get away with it. It's got to be tonight."

Why was everything so urgent? Ever since the caterer got shut down Monday, her life had moved into a new level of out-of-control. She wished she could tell Mike what was going on, get his opinion about what to do. But she knew his answer would be completely subjective—stay and finish the weddings. And she couldn't blame him. If she were in his position, she would say exactly the same thing.

Mike pulled some green latex gloves from a paper bag on the floor. "SpyWizard said you have to be careful with the powder," he said.

"Gee, you'll practically be invisible out there with those neon signs on your hands," she said.

"The hardware store was out of clear ones, so I got these from my dentist."

"Always thinking. Bet you left a real hole in the legal world when you quit that Chicago law firm."

He flashed a mock glare at her and the sparkle in his eyes went straight to her heart.

"Let's concentrate on the conspiracy, shall

we?" he said. "I just wish I'd bought into what you were saying earlier. We might have caught the guy already. You're pretty damn perceptive."

She wondered whether he would be so impressed with her if he knew she was planning to take off in two days, leaving him and all the other heirs high and dry. Guilt tweaked at her conscience.

He pulled a small plastic jar of gray powder and a long-bristled brush from the bag. "Okay, I'll dust the timer. You keep a lookout."

"Maybe we should wait until dark," she said. "So we don't get caught and charged with defacing property or something."

"They close at nine and lock the gates," Mike said. "If we get caught then, it'll be for trespassing *and* defacing property." He reached across the space between their seats and patted her leg. "Ready?"

"As I'll ever be."

They got out of the car and met at the front bumper.

"Let's go. Just act like you belong here."

"Yeah, me and the guy with the green hands."

Mike jammed the gloves, jar and brush in the back pocket of his jeans, then led Delaney

down a stone path that wove through the back
gardens. Even this early in the season, the
beds were spectacular, a stunning mix of
colors and flowers.

"You stay here. If anyone looks like they're
coming my way, stop them." He set off for
the carriage house.

"No problem," she said with more confidence than she felt. She wandered toward a
flower garden designed around a white
statue of a man in a toga. Tipping her head
back, she pretended to study its lines. Out
of the corner of her eye, she spotted a
couple strolling down the path toward her.
As they neared, her mouth moved before
her brain even knew what she was going to
say. "I'm sorry, but the grounds close in
just a few minutes."

"I thought they were open until nine,"
the man said.

"Not on Tuesdays. Tuesdays it's eight-
thirty." Delaney laughed nervously.
"People always get it mixed up. So they
send me out to make sure no one gets
locked in for the night."

"Is the museum closing, too?" he asked.

Is the museum closing, too? She franti-
cally considered her choices. "Actually, it's

open until nine, so feel free to look around inside for the last half hour if you'd like."

They headed toward the museum and Delaney let out a sigh of relief. Where the heck was Mike? How long could it possibly take to brush a little powder on a timer?

A few minutes later a man in a dark business suit came out of the mansion's side door and strode purposefully toward her. Adrenaline shot through her veins. This could be a problem.

"Excuse me," he said when he came close. "Are you the woman telling people the grounds close at eight-thirty?"

Delaney blanched. "You mean they don't?"

"No. Nine o'clock every night." His eyes narrowed and Delaney knew she had to get legitimate fast. Her thoughts tumbled over themselves.

"I'm so sorry. I'm new in town. I shouldn't have spoken without knowing for sure." She stuck out a hand. "I'm Delaney McBride. I've, uh, taken over the Storybook Weddings shop from my late aunt, Ellie Clark. I'm checking out the grounds for photo backdrops for the wedding this weekend."

"Oh. Okay." As he shook her hand, his expression visibly eased. "Ohh. I'm the facilities manager. If you want to call and make an appointment during the day, I can take some time to show you around. Show you some of the more popular photo areas."

"Thank you, I'll do that. But long as I'm here, I'll just finish a quick walk-through right now." She hurried along the path toward the carriage house, heart pounding wildly. Rounding the corner, she almost ran right into Mike.

"Let's go," he said in a low voice, never breaking his stride. He pulled off the gloves and balled the green latex in his fist.

She spun on her heel and raced after him.

Minutes later, they were driving away. He grinned at her. "Mission accomplished."

"Was the timer locked?"

"Nope. Just opened the cover and there it was. Could have changed the times for every day of the week right then if I wanted to."

"Then what took so long?"

"The powder is messy. It was going everywhere. Then I dropped the container and it spilled in the grass, and when I was trying to clean it up, I tore my glove on a rusty clap around the timer conduit." He held up the index finger of his right hand. "This should be purple in no time."

They watched as a violet circle began to

magically appear on the tip of his finger. Delaney started to laugh. "What a pair. I was on the verge of being thrown off the grounds." She described her confrontation with the manager. "So now I have to make an appointment. Like I have time for another meeting." Like there was any point in her having a meeting if she was leaving town.

At the stoplight Mike turned to her and said, "The new caterer will work out fine. By Saturday night, everything will be over and all this new pressure will be gone."

She nodded. Yeah. One way or another, this new pressure would be gone. The question was, would she?

WEDNESDAY NIGHT, top of the ninth, score 6–4, two men on base and two outs. Sitting next to Andy in the stands, Delaney leaned forward, elbows on her knees. "Your dad looks so much like he did in high school right now," she said. In his navy-blue pin-striped jersey, cap pulled low on his forehead against the glare of the lights, Mike oozed self-confidence at second base.

"He says he used to play better," Andy said.

"That double play was pretty impressive. I think they'll be celebrating at Ollie's tonight."

"Are you gonna go?" Andy looked at her sideways.

Delaney shrugged and knew she shouldn't. "I don't know."

"You should. I think my dad wants you to go."

"Yeah?" If only she could figure out a way not to let Mike down—not to let everyone down. "I've got a few worries right now…"

"Everything always works out for the best, my dad says."

Yeah, but getting to the worked-out stage was awful. Delaney watched the batter take his time choosing his pitch, the count going to three balls and one strike before he finally swung and popped up to center. The center fielder positioned himself underneath and waited until the ball fell neatly into his glove, ending the game. Half the crowd erupted in clapping and cheers.

After all the batter's efforts to find the perfect pitch, he'd still ended up getting out.

Kind of felt like her life. The bases were loaded and she was trying to juggle balls and strikes and somehow bring everyone home. And inside she knew, just like the batter, she wasn't going to pull it off.

"Let's go see my dad."

Delaney followed Andy down the bleachers. It was time to accept reality. There wasn't a way to do both things.

Besides, she rationalized, it was unlikely Millie would pull off the wedding dinner, even with Annalisa's help. Once this weekend's bride tasted her food, the odds were zero to none that Delaney would get a passing grade. And even if a miracle occurred and the bride didn't deliver the kiss of death, it was almost a given that the Henrys would. There wasn't enough Jameson in the world to keep them congenial long enough to finish the band shell by the Fourth of July.

Whatever her great-aunt had been trying to do with this will hadn't worked. Her entire estate would go to her brother, which was probably where it should have gone in the first place.

So the decision was made. Delaney would return to her job in Boston and go back to the life she loved, the high-powered advertising world. She swallowed past the tightening in her throat.

"Nice going," Delaney said to Mike. "You guys still have it."

"Thanks. You coming down to Ollie's?"

She shook her head. *I think I'll go home*

and have a cry. "Not tonight. I've got too much to do."

"I'll let you win at pool."

No. She'd made this decision the smart way, without emotion, without giving any weight to the things that had happened between her and Mike. Because those things wouldn't last. And she didn't want to look back later and realize she'd given up everything that mattered to her for a chance with Mike. A chance that never really existed in the first place.

THE MIDDLE OF THE next afternoon, Mike was deep into writing a letter on behalf of a client when Delaney dropped by his office. Dressed in tan capri pants, a black knit shirt and sandals, she was the picture of casual summer.

"Look for the best in legal advice?" he asked with a grin.

Her lips curved up, but the smile didn't reach her eyes. "Do you have a few minutes to take a walk? There's something I want to talk to you about."

"Sure. What's up?"

Delaney shrugged. He followed her out, stopping to tell his administrative assistant he'd be back in half an hour.

They went a block without Delaney saying a word. Finally Mike decided she must be waiting for him to ask. "What's up? Is there another problem with the wedding?"

She avoided his eyes. "How's the car renovation coming along?"

"Well. We'll be done in time for the parade." He waited for Delaney to explain what was going on. As they walked, he looked in the storefronts of the old 1920s stone buildings that lined the downtown street. This was a good town, a comfortable community, an uncomplicated way of life. He was glad he'd come back, for his sake, as well as Andy's. For the first time in a long while, he remembered how his ex-wife had never liked coming here to visit. And how he'd been foolish enough then to think love and a child would overcome any obstacle.

"And the Henrys?"

He sighed. "I'm not sure. The more I try to get a handle on it, the less I seem to learn. Stonewall claims they have it under control."

They stopped at a corner and waited for a couple of cars to pass. Delaney turned to him. "But do they? I was out at the band shell Tuesday and construction hasn't even begun yet."

He winced.

"See, there's the thing," she said. "Even if you restore the car, and even if I manage to pull off a miracle and this new caterer is incredible, the Henrys aren't going to succeed."

"You can't be certain."

"Don't kid yourself. You know it, I know it. The only reason we can't call it a fact yet is because the deadline hasn't passed."

Her unwavering conviction and the edge in her voice gave him pause. "You don't know these guys—"

"I know enough. What they need is a George Patton project manager to oversee them every step of the way. Otherwise they're never going to get there."

"That's pretty judgmental." What was with her attitude this afternoon? "Is something the matter?"

"No. I just don't have time to wait for those two."

"What does that mean? You want to be their project manager *and* the wedding planner?"

She looked into his eyes and he could see she had questions. "No. Not me. I don't have time."

He tried to figure out where this conversation was going.

"My job is important," she said out of the

blue. "Not just to me, but to the company where I work."

"I thought you didn't have a job."

Delaney watched the cars on Main Street, the place where he and Dan would drive the restored Chevy in the Fourth of July parade. Suddenly he realized it no longer mattered whether they were in the parade or not.

"I'm leaving," she said, and he knew the words were coming before they even left her mouth.

"Back to your job."

She nodded.

"Back to the fast lane." He should have known this was coming. Should have known Delaney wouldn't stick it out. The corporate world was too much of a siren call to her.

"The client I lost my job over…they're coming back to the agency and want the same team working for them. The agency needs me."

"There are people who need you here, too."

She turned away. "You don't understand. We're introducing a whole new product line. I need to make a living. And there's no guarantee we'll get the inheritance if I stay. I have to go. I love my job."

She kept talking in that matter-of-fact tone, as though they were discussing taking a vacation and not her leaving Holiday Bay forever. He stared, speechless, fascinated by her ability to rationalize her decision.

"I need to be back in Boston for a flight to Tokyo Saturday, to meet with the top Avalon executives."

"So you're leaving…when?"

"Tonight. I've got a late flight out of Milwaukee."

"And the wedding this weekend? What happens there?" He clenched a fist to keep his anger under control.

She shook her head. "I'm sorry about the wedding, but I don't think my absence will matter. Sooner or later, something would go wrong with a wedding that I couldn't fix and that will be the end. Anyway, the Henrys will never be done in time."

"You won't even try?"

He glimpsed indecision in her expression before she glanced away. "It's not that simple. I need to be at this meeting to show Avalon management that changing agencies for the second time in six months won't result in more marketing turmoil."

"And there's nothing more important than the job."

"Please tell me you understand."

"No. Do what you need to do, Delaney. And justify it any way you want. Just don't ask me to understand."

Her anger flared. "No, I suppose you wouldn't understand someone wanting success in their chosen field. Not when you gave up your career aspirations to live in Holiday Bay."

"Is that what you're calling this? Success?" He laughed bitterly. "You may know a lot about advertising, Delaney, but you have a lot to learn about success."

He walked away and didn't look back. How had he ever thought Delaney anything other than a self-centered woman who only cared about what was in it for her? He should have never let himself get involved.

WHAT DID MIKE WANT from her? Delaney stood at the coffee-shop counter and studied the menu without reading a word. She'd tried. She'd given it her all. No matter how hard she worked, she kept hitting roadblocks.

"What can I get you?"

She jerked her attention to the clerk behind the counter, then focused on the menu again. She needed caffeine so she could stay awake through packing and the three-hour drive to the Milwaukee airport. "A double latte, please."

Every time a roadblock had appeared, she'd climbed over it as best she could. She wanted this inheritance, wanted all of them to get their inheritance. She hated hurting Mike and the others, even the Henrys. But she really needed this job.

Better that they stop pretending *now* that they were going to get an inheritance. Because the Henrys' inability to work together and her uncle's—or someone's— determination to sabotage the wedding made counting on the inheritance too much like gambling in Vegas.

MIKE STOOD IN THE KITCHEN doorway, hands in his pockets, and watched Andy instant- message on the computer with her friends, a chime sounding every time a new message arrived. Her fingers flew over the keyboard and she laughed at a response that came in, oblivious to his presence.

He cleared his throat.

She twisted in her chair. "Daddio! How come you're home from work so early?"

Her personality had seemed to blossom in the past couple of weeks. Sometimes she even did her homework after only being reminded once. He knew it shouldn't be as simple as her working for Delaney, didn't *want* it to be as simple as that. But it was.

And now he had to tell her that Delaney was leaving town. Leaving them all without finishing the job. He had to tell the child he loved that another woman was stepping out of her life, that another woman she cared about put her job first.

"I want to talk to you about something," he said.

Andy's eyes grew round as though she knew an important conversation was coming. She signed off the computer and spun back to face him. "Hey, did Delaney call me about working tomorrow?"

He shook his head.

"She's nice." Andy jumped out of her chair and grabbed a bag of pretzel twists from the cupboard. She flipped off the big plastic clip holding the top closed and took a handful. "And smart, too. I didn't have to work today. I hope she decides to stay here after all the weddings, don't you?"

He nodded slowly. He hadn't let himself think that far ahead, but, yeah, he knew deep down he'd been hoping she would decide to stay. "Honey, I have bad news. Delaney's leaving."

Andy froze with her hand in the bag. She looked up at him with her innocent child's eyes. "How can she leave? There's still weddings to do."

"She got offered her old job back. The advertising agency where she used to work needs her."

"But what about the weddings? What about us?"

The stricken expression on her face cut him like a knife.

"We'll be okay. We'll get by without the inheritance. We didn't have it before, and there's no guarantee we would have gotten it, anyway."

"Not the inheritance, Dad." Andy's voice quavered. "What about *us?*"

He swallowed the lump that lodged in his throat.

"We," he said, "will be fine. She was just the lady who worked at Storybook Weddings for a while. But we've got each other. You and me. We'll always have each other." He wrapped his daughter in his arms.

Andy nodded against his chest. He smoothed her hair and forced away his anger and his hurt and self-recriminations. He should never have let his daughter get so attached to Delaney.

"I thought she liked us," Andy whispered.

"She *does* like us. But her job is important to her. And people have to make decisions that are right for them." After a minute he said, "You want to go out for pizza tonight?"

She shrugged against him.

"And then watch a movie?"

"What about my homework?" There was an touch of sarcasm in her voice. "And don't you have a stupid heirs' meeting tonight?"

Oh, kid, he wanted to say, *screw your homework. Screw the meeting. Tonight we're going to tell the rest of the world to get lost and take some time, just the two of us, to focus on what's important. It wasn't jobs, it wasn't inheritances, and, no, it wasn't homework.*

"How much do you have?" he asked.

"Not too."

He gave her ponytail a tug. "I have to run down to the station to talk to Dan, anyway. Why don't you get started? We'll eat in an hour."

"What about your meeting?"

"With this news, it'll be over quick. Then we'll watch a movie together, okay?"

She wiped the back of her hand across her eyes. "Did she leave because of you?"

"No. She got her old job back."

"It's because you—"

"No, honey. I don't think anyone could have made her stay."

"Love could have."

"Love? It's not that simple." *Not for women like Delaney.*

Andy pushed away from him, her shoulders hunched like a wall between them. "You're even dumber than I thought. I'm going to do my homework."

CHAPTER THIRTEEN

MIKE CLIMBED INTO THE driver's seat of the Chevy and thought about the day he'd driven Delaney out to Sunset Point, the day he realized he'd been kidding himself that he was spending time with her just to ensure she'd stay to do the weddings. He hadn't been able to stop thinking about her ever since.

And now she'd left town.

He started the engine.

Dan walked over and rested his hands on the frame of the open window. "What are you doing?"

"We would have had it restored in time. Ellie would have been proud. Makes no difference anymore whether we drive it in the parade or not. But I thought, with Delaney leaving, I'd take one last spin before we have to turn it over to Lou Waverly. You want to go?"

"What the hell." Dan walked around to the passenger side of the car and got inside.

Five minutes later they were on the open highway, the top down and the radio tuned to an oldies station.

"How's the new baby doing?" Mike asked.

"Slept four hours in a row last night."

"I remember those days. Thought I'd never sleep through the night again."

"Yeah, and now Andy's eleven."

"Going on twenty-nine," Mike said. "She blames me for Delaney leaving."

Dan nodded. "Smart kid, that one."

"I'm not responsible—she took a job."

"She's been nuts about you since she was eight."

"Childhood infatuations don't necessarily translate into adult relationships. Anyway, she wasn't worth the risk." Mike turned the radio down.

Dan snorted. "The risk?"

"Andy and I have a nice, low-key life. It's—"

"Boring." Dan turned his face to the wind coming through the open window.

"Calm, I was going to say. Delaney, on the other hand, is into the corporate ladder and all the stress that comes with it."

"So given a choice, you'd go without love rather than take a risk. Doesn't sound like the Mike I used to know."

"That's not it."

"What is it, then?" Dan tapped his fingers on the armrest.

Mike looked at his friend. "My life is secure and smooth and safe."

Dan smiled. "And predictable."

Predictable? "There's nothing wrong with predictable."

"Not a thing. Unless you like life dull. I just never thought it was your style."

Mike frowned. "Don't muddy the waters. Delaney is a whole other complication. Ever since her arrival, things have been upside down…"

"And?" Dan pressed.

"And?" Mike echoed.

"And, maybe fun?"

Mike narrowed his eyes and opened his mouth to make a quick comeback. But the words died on his tongue as he realized Dan might be right. He thought back to his divorce, to leaving Chicago and coming home to Holiday Bay. Had he been running since his marriage ended?

"So, I repeat," Dan said, a knowing smile

on his face, "you'd go without love rather than take a risk?"

Mike gripped the steering wheel. "Who said anything about love?"

Dan laughed.

"I'm not in love with Delaney," Mike protested.

"Keep telling yourself that. Maybe someday you'll begin to believe it."

Mike shook his head. "I may have been attracted to Delaney, but I can tell you this for sure—I am not in love with her."

Dan just laughed again.

THOUGH SHE HAD HER CAR packed by late afternoon, Delaney struggled to make herself leave. She hadn't told Andy she was going, hadn't even said goodbye to her. But once the conversation with Mike had gone so poorly, she knew she had no business showing up at his house—it would be overstepping of the greatest magnitude.

The phone rang and she quickly picked it up.

"Delaney, this is Annalisa. We have a bit of a problem for Saturday."

Delaney debated whether she should cut the conversation short and just tell the woman she was leaving. "What's wrong?"

"There's been a misunderstanding. When you told me I was to assist Millie with the food preparation, I thought that also meant her staff would be serving at the wedding. But she thought my staff would be serving—"

"Don't tell me."

"Yes. We both told our servers they wouldn't be needed. Now we don't have enough help for the wedding. We've been asking everyone we know, but so far, we're not having much luck. That's why I'm calling you."

If it wasn't one thing with this job, it was another. "Annalisa, I can't help you this time. I'm leaving town in a few minutes, you'll just have to do the best you can. I think Megan Hobart will be handling everything from here on out."

When she finished the call, Delaney reread the notes she'd written for Megan, then let herself out of the shop and locked the door. Guilt and regret nagged at her, but she forced herself to concentrate on the excitement of going back to her job, on the meeting in Tokyo, on working with a client she truly liked, on leaving wedding planning and its problems behind.

She tried not to think about the disappointment her aunt would've felt knowing Delaney had quit.

Her flight left for Boston at ten-thirty; with only a three-hour drive to Milwaukee, she'd have plenty of time to spare. She closed her fist around the keys to the shop.

"What am I supposed to do with these?" she murmured. She certainly didn't want to deliver them to Mike. And she didn't want to give them to Megan and Dan, either. As much as she believed in the integrity of her decision, she wasn't ready to face any of them.

She put a hand against the glass of the Storybook Weddings picture window and flashed back to the day she'd arrived, remembered how much she hadn't wanted to be here. Now, even though she was going toward the future she was meant to have, she was filled with mixed emotions about leaving so soon. About disappointing so many people.

About never seeing Mike again.

As she approached her car, she spotted Andy racing toward her down the sidewalk. Her chest tightened. At least she would be able to say goodbye to the little girl whose company she had come to enjoy so much.

"My dad said you were leaving. Is it true?"
Delaney nodded.

"I wanted to say goodbye and…" Andy stared at the ground and kicked a stone. When she raised her head, her eyes glistened with tears. "And ask if you could stay."

Delaney swallowed hard. She opened her arms and took Andy in. "Sweetheart, thank you. I'm so glad you came. I wish I could stay, but I can't."

"Yes, you can." Andy's voice came out muffled against Delaney's shirt. She pulled back, an obstinate expression on her face. "You can stay if you want to. It's a choice you're making."

"Honey, it's my job. I need to make a living."

"It's your *choice*." Andy pressed her lips together in a hard line and crossed her arms over her chest. "My dad says every time you choose to do something, you're also choosing not to do something else."

"Your dad's a wise man." Regret stabbed at her again.

"Why can't you choose to stay here instead, and choose not to go back there? Why can't you choose to make a living doing weddings?"

Delaney smiled at the naïveté of childhood. "Honey, wedding planning isn't my background. The only thing I know about it is what I've learned in the past three weeks. If my aunt hadn't set up everything in advance, if she hadn't been so organized, I never would have made it this far."

"I would help you."

"I know you would."

"I'm going to miss you. Really a lot." The quaver in Andy's voice betrayed her stoicism.

"I'm going to miss you really a lot, too." Delaney pulled the girl into her arms again.

Andy sniffed and wiped her hand across her nose. She reached into the back pocket of her jean shorts, pulled out a crumpled piece of paper and handed it to Delaney. "This is my e-mail address. Will you write me sometimes?"

"You bet. All the time." She tucked the paper into her purse.

"I put down my phone number and address, too, just in case you want to call or…something."

"Let me give you mine." Delaney tore a deposit slip out of her checkbook and scribbled on it. "There," she said, handing it to Andy. "Now we can both write. Come on, get in the car and I'll drive you home."

Andy slid her hand into Delaney's. Tears sprang to Delaney's eyes now and she blinked hard to hold them back. She squeezed Andy's hand, then let go to pull open the passenger door.

Andy shook her head. "I don't want a ride."

"You sure?"

Andy nodded, her tears beginning to fall. "See you, Delaney." She ran across the street, then yelled over her shoulder, "I love you!"

Delaney watched as the girl ran down the block and rounded the corner, disappearing from sight. "I love you, too," she whispered.

Andy deserved so much more than just an e-mail or phone call every now and then. Delaney drew a shaky breath. She'd be better once she got out of town and even better once she got on the plane. She squeezed the keys in her hand until they dug in to her palm. And she could get out of town as soon as she figured out what to do with these keys.

Since Mike, Dan and Megan were out, it pretty much meant her great-uncle. She didn't feel like facing him, either, but at least she wasn't likely to see disappointment in *his* eyes. He'd probably be overjoyed to learn she was pulling out.

Five minutes later she took the stairs two at a time to his second-floor office, intending to deliver the keys and get out. Except the door was locked. She twisted the knob irritably; just her luck that he was already gone for the day.

Suddenly the door opened and Claire stood in the doorway. "Delaney? I was just locking up."

Blue, the humping poodle, came charging down the hall straight for Delaney. She stuck a foot out and held the dog off. "Is my uncle around?"

"He's meeting with his financial adviser."

Well, wasn't this fortuitous? After he got all their inheritances, he'd have plenty more to discuss with the guy.

Claire pointed at the clock on her desk. "They should be out soon. Lou has to be somewhere else in half an hour. Can you wait?" She went back to her desk and began to sort through some papers.

Delaney debated her answer. She wasn't looking forward to telling Uncle Lou she was leaving, didn't want to see his triumph when he realized he'd won. On the other hand, if she was wrong about him being the saboteur, she didn't want to leave town without saying goodbye.

"I'll wait a few minutes." She took a seat and picked up last week's *Time* magazine from the end table. Moments later, Blue was back wrapping his paws around her bare calf.

Delaney tried to gently shake him off, and when that didn't work, she reached down to force him away with her hand. "No!" she said in the lowest, sternest voice she could muster.

He cocked his head as though appraising the seriousness of her command, then wandered over to Claire and plopped down beside her desk. Jeez, she should have tried the alpha-male thing three weeks ago.

Lou's office door opened and he came out with another man. "I'll check the viability of those companies and get back to you next week," the financial adviser said as he crossed the office.

As soon as the door closed behind the man, Lou turned to Delaney. "Well, hello," he said, smiling. "Is this a social visit or is there something I can do for you?"

This guy was either the best actor in the world or they were wrong about him. She was glad she'd decided to say goodbye, just in case. She stood and put her purse over her shoulder. "I don't know if you heard... Probably not, since I just told Mike a couple of hours ago."

He raised his eyebrows.

"I've been rehired at my old job. The account I used to work on is coming back to the ad agency and I have to be at a meeting in Tokyo next week. We fly out Saturday morning."

"You're leaving?" Uncle Lou's forehead furrowed. "Without finishing?"

"Don't you have a wedding to do this weekend?" Claire asked in a high voice.

Delaney nodded. "I tried to figure out a way to make everything work, but I can't. I left notes for Megan so she can finish everything up."

"But you'll lose your inheritance," Claire said.

"I don't have a choice. I've been out of work for over three months. I need this job."

Uncle Lou's expression didn't change. "That's too bad. We'll be sorry to see you go. But I understand."

Well. He sure wasn't making any effort to convince her to stay, was probably already drinking champagne in his mind. Claire seemed more concerned about Delaney losing her inheritance than Uncle Lou did. "I forgot to give Mike the keys to the shop and apartment. That's why I stopped by. Could I leave them with you?" She handed them to her uncle and they disappeared into his big fist.

"I'll really sorry you can't stay," he said, giving her a hug. "Keep in touch."

Yeah, right.

Claire came out from behind the desk to give Delaney a hug, as well. "Best of luck to you. Let us know how you're doing," she said.

When Delaney finally got back into her car, she was hit by an overwhelming relief that it was all over. This town held nothing for her anymore. No hopes, no dreams, no future. She headed for the highway, passing familiar landmarks along the way—the grade school, the old ice-cream parlor, the gas station on the corner, the fire station, the road to the old cemetery where they used to ride their bikes, the city-limit sign, freshly painted in clean blue and gray: Thank you for visiting Holiday Bay.

"Thanks for having me," she murmured. The last time she'd even noticed that sign, she and her mother had been moving out of town. Delaney had sobbed when her mother said, "Before too long, you'll forget all about Holiday Bay and feel the same way about the next place we live." At that moment she'd hated her mother and decided she would never love anywhere like this again because it hurt way too much when you left.

"Thank you for visiting." In how many different cities and towns had she seen those words when she was leaving? In how many

hotels and restaurants? In how many relationships—friends, lovers, coworkers—had
it been implied?

Too many. She punched the radio button
and rock music flooded the car, burying her
pain beneath its throbbing rhythm. Anything
to keep her thoughts occupied so she didn't
have room in it to think.

Thanks for visiting. The phrase crept into
her brain like dust blown off a newly plowed
field seeps beneath closed windows.

She hadn't held true to her vow to never
love again. She had loved more than one
man, more than one city, but each time
always less than the last.

She'd always been just a visitor.

Tears blinded her and she pulled the car to
the side of the road and put on the flashers.
When had it happened? When had she
become a visitor instead of a permanent
resident? She searched her mind, but couldn't
find any definitive moment. Just a series of
decisions—choices, Andy called them—that
kept taking her away from belonging
anywhere or with anyone. Choices to not get
involved, to not care. Choices that were, on
the flip side, decisions to stay separate,
remain alone.

From the moment she'd learned about this will, she hadn't wanted to take it on. Long ago she'd learned not to count on anyone but herself; it just made life easier. The will put her in an odd place—relying on others for her inheritance and, ultimately, happiness, and all these people relying on her.

It had scared her. What did you owe people who relied on you? And if they came through for you, what did you owe them? Your life? Happiness?

And what if you couldn't deliver?

She closed her eyes and let the tears fall. She'd spent the past fifteen years making sure she didn't make the same mistakes as her mother.

But was her life really any different? Or any better? She didn't belong anywhere—or with anyone. No close friends except her coworkers, and even they were more associates than friends. She had a job in Boston—but not any real loyalty to the city.

Flashing red and blue lights reflected in her rearview mirror and she looked over her shoulder to see a sheriff's department squad car on the shoulder behind her. *Just great.*

She reached for the door handle, intending to jump out and tell him nothing was wrong, but stopped herself at the last second. She'd heard cops didn't like it when people did that—made them nervous, as if you might have a gun or something. She dragged a hand across her eyes to wipe all trace of her tears, then smiled at the burly officer through the open window.

"Everything okay here?" the man asked.

Delaney nodded. "Yes. Just—just not sure which way I want to go."

"Where you headed? I can give you directions."

If only it were that simple. Her shoulders sagged. "You probably can't help me. I'm headed for Boston. But I'm not so sure where I'm going."

The deputy's face stayed expressionless. "That's a long way to travel without knowing where you're going. Maybe you oughta stop at the next town and get yourself a map. Plot your course, figure out where you want to stop and rest along the way."

"Thanks." She forced a smile.

"You'll get where you're going with a lot less hassle. Maybe even enjoy the trip. Good luck."

Delaney watched him in the side mirror as he went back to the squad car. "Thanks, but I have a map already," she murmured. And that's what seemed to be the problem. She'd made no room for detours, sightseeing or adventures along the way. No room to discover if there was something out there other than what she'd already chosen. No time to find out if what she'd chosen was what she really wanted.

She hit the butt of her hand against the steering wheel.

And what difference did it make knowing all that about herself? She still needed to make money. And she had an incredible job offer waiting in Boston that would turn her life around.

She could stop being a visitor there.

She could stay with that job for a long time. Could make an effort to get to know her co-workers better. Could volunteer somewhere and make friends outside work.

Except she was leaving her fellow heirs high and dry.

Delaney slumped into her seat. She might end her visiting days in Boston, but she wanted to leave Holiday Bay full of friends. She wanted to help the others get their inheritances. She wanted to see the expressions on their faces when they knew they'd all succeeded.

What was she thinking? She couldn't go back to Holiday Bay. If she stayed to finish the weddings, she would have to give up the job. She'd have to keep flying trapeze without a net. And she'd still have all the other problems with the catering staff, the Henrys and someone trying to sabotage the weddings.

She swallowed hard and thought of the Henrys' decision-making method. Pros and cons. If both options had the potential to cause harm, then the best choice had to be the one that caused the least amount of damage. The ad agency would probably get the account back whether she was there or not. But there was no way the heirs would get their inheritances if she left.

Maybe the ad agency would understand if she called and explained the situation. Maybe they would hold the job a few weeks if she told them what was at stake—not just for her, but for the others. And if not, well…

She nodded to herself. She'd made a commitment to do the weddings. She owed it to her fellow heirs. *Her friends.* It was the right thing to do.

So now what?

"Take charge, Delaney," she said softly. "Take charge." She pulled out onto the road and drove a few more miles, until suddenly, before she even knew she'd made a decision, she'd done a U-turn. She looked at her hands on the steering wheel and grinned. "Nice job, guys."

Her smile faded. What the hell was wrong with her fingers? She turned her right hand palm up and examined it. Every finger was partially stained purple.

How did she get ink all over her hand? She pulled onto the shoulder again, dug a wet wipe out of the glove compartment and tried to clean off her fingers. The purple got darker. She frowned. If she didn't know better... She dropped the wet wipe on the floor. If she didn't know better, she would think she'd gotten into the detection powder. Except they'd been in Mike's car, not hers, when they did the job. So how the heck had she gotten this all over her—

Calf?

She touched the purple stain on her lower right leg. Her heart started to hammer.

The dog. Her uncle. *The dog.* The detection powder Mike spilled in the grass. He said the stuff spread— Oh, no! She popped down the visor to look in the vanity mirror; a violet stripe meandered across her eyelids. "Beautiful. That's what I get for crying."

She couldn't wait to tell Mike. Tell him? He'd see it for himself.

She shoved the gearshift into Drive and jammed her foot down on the accelerator. After a minute, she eased up. Didn't need to get a speeding ticket from the deputy she'd just met.

As the miles rolled away under her tires, she turned her focus to the upcoming wedding. They still needed servers. Heck, she'd wait tables if it would help. Mike and Dan could serve. And the Henrys—there were two of them. Knowing Megan, she'd probably insist on helping, too. That made six right there. Maybe forcing the Henrys to work together in public…

She grinned. Another problem almost solved. The first thing she'd do when she got back to town, even before talking to Mike, would be to call Annalisa.

She passed the Welcome to Holiday Bay sign and said, "Damn glad to be here!" Then she drove past her uncle's office and held herself back from hanging out the window and shouting, *You can't get rid of Delaney McBride that easily!* They were probably gone already anyway.

Hell, they had her keys.

She parked her car in front of Storybook Weddings and called information from her cell phone to get Annalisa's number. As soon as the woman answered, Delaney launched into her plan.

"But what if they say no?" Annalisa asked.

"Don't let yourself worry about that for a minute. You just get ready to cook. I'll talk to everyone and call you back when I have your serving staff finalized." She closed her phone. This was getting to be fun.

She looked at her purple fingers. And the fun wouldn't end anytime soon. Because now she needed to tell Mike about her uncle. *She needed to tell Mike she was back.* And she needed to tell Andy. If she was lucky, both would be at home right now.

Ten minutes later she was standing on Mike's front porch in the waning daylight, hands on her hips in frustration. No one was home. They weren't at the service station, either—she'd driven past it on the way here and the lights were off. She couldn't believe she had the best news ever and no one to share it with. She sighed. They could be anywhere right now. She supposed she could call Mike's cell phone, but she'd much rather surprise him in person. She glanced at her watch. Just past seven.

The heirs' meeting. Mike was in the library at the Thursday-night heirs' meeting.

Exactly where she was supposed to be, too.

He'd probably already told them she'd skipped town. They were probably talking about it right now, hating her at this very minute.

And rightfully so.

This was *really* getting to be fun.

MIKE WAITED PATIENTLY for the dull roar to subside.

"What do you mean, she quit?" Sully asked. "Get her back."

"Can't. She's left town already."

"She told you, then took off? All in the same day?" Stonewall slouched down into his chair, disgusted. "I knew this thing was never going to work."

"We saw her Tuesday and she said she had to figure some things out. Just thought it had to do with weddings," Sully said.

"Guess she figured them out." Mike tamped down the anger that welled up inside him every time he devoted more than five seconds to thinking about Delaney quitting.

"Didn't she care about what this meant for everyone else?" Sully asked.

"To be honest, Sully, I think she figured you two were the ones who didn't care what happened."

"Us?"

Mike exchanged a look with Dan. "You were always bickering so much, she figured you'd never get the band shell built in time."

"I cared," Sully said.

"Me, too." Stonewall nodded. "We've always disagreed—"

"Yeah, but it didn't mean we weren't friends."

"Right."

"Guys, it's a little late for a lovefest," Dan said. "With Delaney gone, you can keep fighting till the day you die and it won't matter."

"So now you boys won't get the car or the money." Sully shook his head.

"We'll be okay. It's not like we already had it and lost it," Mike said.

"I just can't believe Delaney didn't need a hundred thousand dollars." Stonewall pulled absently at one of his eyebrows. "It's a lot of money to walk away from."

"I think she felt she was in a corner. And had to make a choice." Mike stood and crossed the room. "Things kept going wrong with the wedding planning. When the caterer was shut down, she figured the handwriting was on the wall."

"Didn't seem like the quitting type," Sully said. "She seemed like a fighter to me."

Mike shrugged. "Appearances," he said slowly, "can sometimes be deceiving."

DELANEY REACHED THE LIBRARY and raced up the stairs to the second floor, drawing up short at the sight of the brown-haired girl bent over her homework at a big wooden table just outside the meeting room. She swallowed hard. "Hey, Andy," she whispered.

Andy raised her head. Suddenly her eyes rounded. She started to stand, then stopped herself. "Did you forget something? What's that on your eyes?"

"I came back to do the weddings. And my eyes? I'll tell you all about it later." She bent to kiss the top of Andy's head.

Andy clapped her hands together. "Wait till my dad hears this. He's been pretty crabby all night."

"He has? Then I'd better get in there and change his mood, don't you think?"

CHAPTER FOURTEEN

THE DOOR BURST OPEN and banged against the opposite wall. Every head spun round to see what was going on. Delaney stood in the doorway like a conquering hero. *Hell, like Xena, the warrior princess,* Mike thought. The only thing missing was the skimpy outfit. Although the purple stripe across her eyes was a nice touch. And the shade seemed familiar… He inspected the stain on the tip of his right index finger.

Same color.

What had Delaney been up to the past couple of hours?

"Seems like a fighter to me, too," Stonewall muttered.

Delaney strode toward the table, then fixed her gaze on each of the men in turn. "Gentlemen."

Andy leaned in the door to give Mike a thumbs-up. He grinned back at her.

No one so much as breathed. Even the air in the room seemed to hang utterly still in anticipation. Andy sneaked inside and sat in the corner by the whiteboard to watch.

Delaney scowled at the Henrys, and the two actually had the good sense to look afraid. As angry as he was with her for what she'd pulled earlier today, Mike felt a grudging admiration for the entrance she'd just made and the effect she was having on the men.

"I have a wedding to do this weekend." Delaney leaned forward to rest her hands on the table. "You've probably heard about the caterer being shut down. That's old news. I'm already onto a new crisis and I'm going to need everyone's help." She straightened.

"Anything you want," Stonewall said.

"We're here for you," Sully added.

Delaney hesitated, momentarily caught off balance by their remarks. She quickly recovered. "We have a shortage of servers for the wedding dinner. I need everyone to wait tables if we're going to pull this thing off and get a satisfactory rating." She pointed at each of the men in turn. "That means everyone."

"Yeah. Sure. Absolutely. No problem."

The words tumbled out of them, one on top of the other.

Delaney's expression softened. A smile broke across her face, and her quiet laugh warmed Mike's heart. He didn't know what had brought her back, but he was glad she'd come.

"I can work, too," Megan said. "At least for a couple of hours."

"That would be fantastic." Delaney raised her arms as though drawing everyone into a big hug. "All of you. Thank you. You're wonderful."

"No. Thank *you*," Sully said. "You're the one who's wonderful. We've been…well, less than that."

"I'm not so sure about that. I know vinegar way too well and have a lot to learn about honey." Her voice caught.

"Honey can be overrated," Stonewall said. "Sometimes what's needed is a dose of vinegar to clean off the mineral deposits and get the mechanism moving again."

"And who would know that better than you?" Sully muttered, standing.

Delaney laughed and started for the door. "I'd better call the caterer and tell her we've got all the help she needs."

"Meeting adjourned," Sully said loudly. He gave Mike a shove in the back. "This time, don't wait so long to go after her."

Mike chased Delaney out the door, almost crashing into her in the hall when she stopped and whirled around. Her face registered her surprise.

"Hi," he said. He took a step back.

"Uh, hi. Hey, didn't you tell me you have an extra set of keys to the wedding shop and apartment?"

"Yeah, they're at my house."

"I need to get those. I gave mine to my uncle." Delaney set off again.

Mike took two steps to catch up with her. "Why'd you do that?" he asked, when what he wanted to say was, *You're incredible.*

"Stupidity. Sheer stupidity."

No, you're the most intelligent woman I know. "So, uh, what's with the stripe across your eyes?"

"I'll give you one guess. It's not mascara." Delaney showed him her hands.

"Weren't you listening when I told you how easily that stuff spreads? So where'd you get it? Did you go back to the Dalton House?"

She rolled her eyes. "I'll tell you everything outside. You're going to love it."

They went down the stairs side by side. "Hey, thanks for coming back," Mike said. "I'm really glad you're here."

"Me, too." She smiled.

"What about your job?"

"Yeah, I've got to call them tomorrow." She scrunched up her face.

"They don't know you're not coming?" Andy dashed up beside them, backpack slung over her shoulder.

Delaney shook her head. "Not yet."

"Will they be mad?" Andy asked.

"Probably. They were depending on me. But people here were depending on me, too. And you know what?" She tousled Andy's hair. "I care a lot more about the people here than the ones there."

Mike wanted to wrap her in his arms and hold her tight. Instead, he put an arm around her shoulders. "I think you've mastered the honey-vinegar-ratio thing."

She grinned and pushed through the door outside. "Check out my right calf."

He'd already checked out both her legs weeks ago, but okay, if she insisted, he'd force himself to do it again. The purple had stained her lower leg. "You're covered with the stuff."

"Why do you have purple all over you?" Andy asked.

"I dropped my keys off at my uncle's office, remember?"

"Yeah. And?" Mike said.

"The dog."

Mike cocked his head. "The dog? What? He wanted your leg?" As he looked at the stain on Delaney's calf again, all the dots connected. *I spilled the powder in the grass.*

Delaney nodded knowingly. "The dog."

"Hot damn." Mike punched a triumphant fist in the air. "Well, if it's on the dog, it's on Lou's fingers. We've got that son of a bitch. Want to pay a visit in the morning?"

Delaney unlocked her BMW. "I'm right there with you. I'll follow you home to get the keys. Then, I'm going to unpack so we can hit the ground running tomorrow."

"Why does Delaney have purple all over her?" Andy fell into step beside Mike as they headed to their car.

"It's a long story. I'll tell you on the way home," he said. "Come on, we've got a movie to watch."

God, he was glad Delaney was here. He hadn't fully appreciated how much he would miss her until she'd returned. Now he didn't ever want to let her go again. Suddenly, it hit him; Dan had been right. Somehow, in the past three weeks, he'd fallen in love with Pumpkin McBride.

"THE PURPLE IS LIGHTER on your face this morning." Mike stopped on the sidewalk outside Lou Waverly's building and peered under Delaney's baseball cap.

"Thank goodness. It must be because it's a third-hand stain. From the dog to my fingers to my face." Delaney tugged the cap lower on her forehead. "What if we're wrong about my uncle? What if he just took the dog for a walk?"

"At the Dalton House? A museum that doesn't allow pets on the grounds? Unlikely. Still, that's why we're not going to accuse him outright. We're just getting the keys back for you."

"Right." Delaney fiddled with the cap again. "If my uncle's guilty, I want to catch him. But I hope we find out he isn't. I'm glad Aunt Ellie's not here to see this. It would devastate her."

"Don't cross too many bridges too soon." Mike locked his fingers around hers. "Let's go."

When they entered Lou's office, Claire looked up in surprise, hands frozen at the computer keyboard. "Delaney? I thought you'd left."

"I hardly got out of town before I changed my mind," Delaney said.

A moment later Uncle Lou stepped into the reception area, Blue dancing around his feet. "Did I just hear Delaney out here? What brings you back?"

She tried to read his reaction. Happy and delighted? Or surprised and suspicious? Lou stuffed his hands into his pockets and Delaney's stomach dropped. *Oh, Uncle Lou.*

"She changed her mind," Mike said just as she said, "I didn't like running out on my obligations."

Blue zeroed in on Mike and began to jump excitedly at his legs. Delaney swallowed a laugh. Better him than her.

"That's good. Very good," Lou said. "So what about the new job? They'll wait for you?"

"I don't think so. My guess is the job will go to someone else."

"We just stopped to pick up the keys so she can get back into the shop." Mike glowered at the dog and pushed him away with his foot.

"Blue! Bed!" Lou barked. The poodle slunk away down the hall.

Lou went into his office and returned with the keys. As he neared Delaney, a frown furrowed his brow and he bent to look under the rim of her cap. "You've got purple across your eyes."

"Yeah, I know."

"It's the same stuff I have all over my fingers." Lou held up his hands. "What is it? I thought maybe it was from changing the cartridge in the printer. But when I tried to wash it off, it just spread."

"Detection powder," Mike said slowly. "From the timer for the outdoor sprinkler system at the Dalton House."

"What are you talking about?" Lou asked.

"We think someone's been trying to sabotage the weddings," Delaney explained. "And we were afraid they might try to set the sprinkler to go off during Saturday's wedding. So we put detection powder on the timer."

"It's invisible until it mixes with the skin's natural oil, then it stains purple. Pretty much nothing will remove it," Mike added.

He sounded so proud of himself, Delaney half expected him to pull out a decoder ring and spy-club membership card.

"But I haven't been anywhere near the Dalton House, let alone the timer for their sprinkler system." Lou frowned. "So how did it get all over me?"

"The same way it got all over me," Delaney said. "Your dog. Mike spilled the powder on the ground by the timer. That's where Blue got into it. I touched your dog yesterday and now my hands are stained. Look what happened where he was hanging on to my calf." Delaney pulled up her pant leg.

"You think I would try to ruin a wedding? Make sure you don't succeed?" He spoke so sadly, Delaney wished she and Mike were wrong.

"You get the entire inheritance if the heirs fail." She couldn't bring herself to say, *You're the only one with motive.*

"No, I don't. There's more to this will than you realize. Only Ellie, her attorney and I know the extent of it."

"More?" Mike, Delaney and Claire said together.

Exactly how much more could her aunt have come up with? Hadn't she already made life difficult enough?

"There's a codicil to the will. I know I should have brought it forward before now."

Lou drew a slow breath. "Ellie asked me not to reveal it until your deadline had passed."

"July Fourth," Delaney said.

"I guess I should start at the beginning," Lou said. "Ellie wanted to leave a legacy of the love she and Henry shared. Of the friendships they had with special people in this town." He crossed the reception area and turned back to face them. "We discussed a lot of ways for her to leave that legacy. It started with the car. She wanted the Chevy restored because it was the car Henry courted her in. That's what made her think of assigning duties to each heir."

"But how did *I* get in there?" Delaney asked. "I didn't live here. I hadn't had much contact with her in years."

"When Mike moved back after his divorce, Ellie decided what he needed was to love again, to find the kind of relationship she and Henry had."

"She actually talked to me about that," Mike said.

Lou touched Delaney on the shoulder. "She remembered you once had feelings for Mike. And she deduced during your visits here that you didn't have a lot of faith in the longevity of love." He shrugged and smiled sheepishly. "So she set up her will to throw you and Mike together and hoped sparks would fly. Not her business, but what are you going to do with a romantic old woman?" His smile faded. "As for the Henrys, you've probably figured this out already. She wanted them to learn to get along without Henry Clark to mediate."

"Dan and I suspected as much about the Henrys," Mike said.

Lou paced toward them, hands still in his pockets. "She had fun putting this together. But she didn't want anyone to actually lose out if they couldn't accomplish what she'd asked."

Claire frowned. "But the will says—"

"That's the will. The codicil the attorney drew up, the one that I have, gives all heirs their inheritances whether they meet the terms of the will or not."

Delaney gasped.

"Damn," Mike said.

Claire sank back into her chair, clearly shocked.

"You mean the weddings don't…the band shell…the '57 Chevy…we all get…" Delaney couldn't formulate a coherent thought.

"No. Yes. Whatever the question. The bottom line is, she loved all of you very much. And no matter what happened, she wanted to make sure you had something to remember her by."

He looked from Delaney to Mike. "She loved all of you too much to pull the rug out from under you like that."

"Oh, Uncle Lou, I'm sorry about all this," Delaney said.

"But then, why is there detection powder all over Blue?" Mike asked.

Hearing his name, the poodle stole back into the room and wagged his tail as if he knew he was in trouble.

Lou looked at Claire. And Claire started to cry. "It's possible," she said in a small voice, "that someone might have taken Blue for some exercise yesterday morning. And that person may have considered changing the timer." Her voice quavered. "That person may have stood there for a long time thinking about what to do. And then decided it was wrong and didn't do anything at all."

Nobody moved a muscle.

Claire held out her hands, not a speck of purple on them. "I didn't touch the timer."

"But why did you even think about changing it?" Lou asked.

"For you. So you could get the inheritance

that should have been yours. So you don't have to face bankruptcy."

"I'm not going bankrupt."

"You're not?" Claire's eyes widened. "But you're always fussing with your accounts, always worried about what's happening in the market. We've been dating for eleven years, three months and four days. And you always say you don't want to get married until things are better."

"You almost ruined a wedding because you thought I was going bankrupt?" he asked.

"Two weddings," Delaney said softly. "Almost ruined two."

Lou jerked his head up. "What do you mean?"

"The thermostat in the florist's cooler was turned down so low all the flowers froze for the second wedding. And the wedding cake got canceled." She kept her eyes on her uncle. "And a few days ago someone anonymously reported the caterer for this Saturday's wedding to the Department of Health and got her shut down for having an unlicensed facility."

Lou glowered at Claire. "You did all this?"

"I thought you were in trouble, that you needed money." Claire's voice shook and tears streaked down her cheeks. "When the soloist for the first wedding got laryngitis, it made me think. What if Delaney didn't get a passing grade from one of the brides? If she failed at wedding planning, you would get the money and your problems would be over."

"But, Claire, I own lots of property, several office buildings. You know that."

"That didn't mean you weren't having problems. How would I know, anyway? You never tell me anything about your finances." She pulled a tissue from her top drawer and blew her nose.

Delaney gaped at Claire, incredulous.

Lou let loose with a huge belly laugh. "I fuss about my accounts because I want them to be right. And when I say I want things to be better, I'm talking about me. I need to feel right about marrying a woman so much younger than I am. I've been through a lot, been a bachelor a long time. I'm pretty set in my ways."

"You know I don't care about any of that," Claire said.

Lou put an arm around her shoulder. "I should be furious at you. What you did was stupid and selfish and expensive. Either I make restitution or you go to jail."

"I'm so sorry," Claire whispered.

"I am, too," he said. "I've been taking care

of myself so long, I never realized you might worry about me. Never realized I wasn't communicating very well. But, honey, you've got to ask if you have questions." He kissed her cheek. "If I marry you, will you stop getting such ideas?"

Her eyes widened and she nodded.

"Okay. Let me check my financial situation and I'll get back to you."

All four of them burst into laughter.

"WAIT UNTIL DAN AND Megan find out about the codicil," Mike said.

"I still can't believe it." Delaney unlocked the door to the wedding shop. "We get our inheritance no matter what. I wish my aunt were here so I could hug her."

"Or yell at her. I'm not sure which."

Delaney nodded. "If we'd only known, I wouldn't have had to come back. I could have had the job of my dreams and the money from Aunt Ellie. Kind of like winning the lottery."

Mike chuckled. He felt as if he'd won the lottery, too, but for him it had happened the moment Delaney entered the heirs' meeting last night. He wanted to tell her how he felt, but there was time enough for that later. Now he'd just revel in the fact that she'd given up the job to come back; the fast life must not have the hold on her that he'd thought it did. "To think I wouldn't have had to worry about the Henrys and weddings for the past few weeks," he said.

"And I wouldn't have had to deal with all those half-crazed perfectionist brides and their mothers." Delaney grinned. "Although it was sort of fun."

"Am I hearing this right? Delaney McBride is admitting to enjoying wedding planning?" He dropped onto one of the stools at the worktable in the back room. "Hey, what did the agency say when you told them you weren't taking the job?"

For a moment her face was blank. Then her jaw dropped in amazement. "I forgot to call. I was so focused on going to see my uncle this morning, I forgot all about it. *They still think I'm coming.*"

"You'd better let them know quickly so they can make other plans," Mike said.

"Mike! Now they don't need to!" She raised her hands and looked upward as though thanking the heavens. "My forgetting to call is a godsend. If I get a flight to Boston today, I can still make the Tokyo flight tomorrow. It doesn't matter *who* finishes out the weddings.

I don't have to give up my job. I can still be the account exec for Avalon." She pulled the Yellow Pages out of the lower drawer of the desk and flipped to the airlines section.

He gaped at her. He'd thought Delaney's decision to turn down the job and finish the weddings meant she'd made decisions about her life, where she was going, what was important. Thought she'd begun to see Holiday Bay—and maybe him—as things worth holding on to.

"Why don't you stay?" he asked.

"What?" She lifted her head to look at him.

"Why don't you stay here?"

"In Holiday Bay? And do weddings?" She crinkled her nose and shook her head. "It's been fun…sometimes. But I think I just got my second chance. Karma or something. Fate telling me I was missing out on what my future was supposed to be and, here, take another shot at it."

"Your aunt worked hard to throw us together. Maybe that's karma, too."

She squinted at him in confusion. "I didn't think we were more than a passing moment. You had your life here. I had my life there. I didn't expect more because, well, I have aspirations. I know you have aspirations, too, but they aren't… I'm sorry, I don't mean that the way it sounds."

If he wanted to, he supposed he could feel offended by her words. Instead, all he felt was disappointment. Fancy titles and lots of money no longer impressed him. What he appreciated now was a comfortable living, a stable home for his daughter, an unrushed lifestyle. He'd found that here. The only thing that would make it better would be a woman to share it with. *Delaney.*

But she wanted something else entirely.

"Don't worry about it," he said. "I'm sure plenty of people think that because I left a big Chicago law firm, I ran away from success. I don't really care. I'm a lot happier now than I was then."

"I'm glad."

He slid off the stool and stepped toward her, wanting only to take her in his arms and convince her to stay. "You'd be happy here, too. So stay. You've done a great job with the planning. You've got the Henrys working together. And…"

"And?" She tilted her head.

"I know Andy wishes you would. Dan and Megan, too." He paused. "*I* wish you would stay."

She stared at him a minute, started to raise her hands in a gesture of supplication before letting them fall to her sides. "I could visit."

Delaney was still chasing bigger, better, more. It was time to move on. "Visiting is always nice." He bent to kiss her lightly on the mouth. "Just remember, there's more to life than just making a living. Good luck in Tokyo, Delaney McBride. I'm going to miss you." More than she would ever know.

DELANEY STOOD THERE holding the phone book and watched him leave, watched him head down the street in the direction of Dan's service station. Stood there while confusion crowded her mind and she tried to sort out what had just happened and what she really wanted. She'd been given a second chance to make her mark in advertising. Opportunities like this were rare—and second chances even more so.

She could visit Mike anytime she wanted.

Visit. The way she had with every relationship, every job, every town in her life. She'd gone down this road yesterday and found it empty. Why did she think the path so much better today?

Especially when Mike was asking her to stay.

Her brain churned and her stomach roiled. She could have the job and the inheritance. She could have the title, the prestige, the money. She could quit being visitor, have friends and a settled life, everything she ever wanted—in Boston.

Except Mike.

Except Andy.

Except wedding planning.

Oh, Lord, she actually liked wedding planning.

Suddenly, leaving Holiday Bay seemed like the worst decision she'd ever made in her life. Mike had asked her to stay. But she didn't just want to be a visitor in his life.

She wanted the fairy tale.

Leaving the keys on the worktable and the door unlocked, she ran outside and started jogging toward Hobart & Hobart Garage and Service Station. By the time she got there, she was sweating. No wonder. Probably eighty degrees already.

She stopped to catch her breath. This was it. Everything was coming out now. Whatever was going on between her and Mike was being laid on the table today. The overhead garage doors were open, and she spotted Mike and Dan standing next to a car, talking.

Stomach fluttering, she entered the garage, her footsteps on the cement floor announcing her arrival.

Mike turned. "Delaney?"

His eyes met hers and her pulse quickened. Every word she'd thought to say evaporated from her mind.

"Um, do you need something?" Dan asked in the awkward silence.

Eyes still locked on Mike's, she shifted her feet, suddenly terrified of the pending conversation. "Oil change," she blurted. "I need an oil change."

"You need an oil change?" Mike lifted a brow.

Tell him. She opened her mouth. "And a filter, too," came out.

"We're booked solid. It'll be a while," Dan said.

"I don't think you have time to wait," Mike added.

"Sure. I can wait. Doesn't need to be today. Next week will be soon enough." Her voice trembled and she clenched her teeth together to keep her jaw steady.

"How are you getting to the airport, then?" Dan asked.

She didn't answer, just looked at Mike. Just watched him watch her.

Dan cleared his throat and took a few steps backward. "I guess I'll go…and organize the, uh, job orders for today. In the office. If you, uh, need me or anything."

When he was gone, Mike asked, "How *are* you getting to the airport?"

"Well…" She waved a hand. "It's just that I'm not going to the airport. Not anymore."

He waited, his eyes never leaving her face.

"Maybe we should take a walk," she said.

"I don't know. The last time you asked me to take a walk, I didn't like the news."

She huffed. "Humor me."

Five minutes and a couple of blocks later, Delaney finally got up the nerve. "I've… It's just there's so many people who need help planning their weddings."

Mike nodded.

"I don't want to leave them in the lurch." She cut through the park and onto a narrow path in the woods, the same path she'd chased him down on many a childhood summer day.

Mike fell into step behind her.

"The thing is, I've visited a lot of places in my life. Places and relationships. And it's getting old," she said over her shoulder.

"Always on the outside looking in," Mike said.

She nodded, even though he couldn't see her face. "And it didn't matter before. It didn't. Until you kissed me."

"Delaney…"

She stopped beside a big old maple tree. "And I may be about as dumb as I can possibly be to even think that what we have could be real, because my mother, you know, spent a whole lifetime searching." She looked up at the canopy of green above them. "I heard something once, something like, marriage kills love and—"

"Are we talking about love here?"

She brought her eyes to his. *Were* they? Her heart pounded. This was her moment of truth. *She* was talking about love. What if he wasn't? What if he'd asked her to stay and he was just talking about lust or friendship?

She pressed a hand to her chest. "I don't want to belong just anywhere. I want to belong with you."

He didn't say anything.

"I can't leave…because I love you." Her voice sped up. "Unless, of course, you don't love me, then, no problem, I can leave…in complete mortification, just like when I was seventeen." She glanced at the path behind them, her cheeks beginning to burn.

Mike started to laugh, then stopped. "Delaney, I can't say whether you belonged with me when you were seventeen. But I can tell you this—you belong with me now."

A wide smile broke across her face. "I do?"

He pulled her into his arms and kissed her. "I love you," he murmured against her mouth.

"Do you know recognize this tree?" She pointed up at the maple.

He winced. "Yeah. The one Dan and I left you tied to for three hours when you were eight."

"But you came back for me." Her voice caught. "Will you always? No matter what? Will you always come back for me?"

"Count on it." He kissed her again. "Now, about that wedding-planning business…"

Delaney rested her hands on his chest. "If I'm going to make a go of it, I've got to book some more weddings."

"I know one you could get started on right away. They haven't picked a date yet, but you could help with that, too."

"Who?"

"All I know is, the wedding has to be filled

with enchantment because that's what brought them together."

He couldn't possibly be saying what she hoped he was saying. "It sounds perfect for Storybook Weddings! Who's getting married?"

He dropped kisses on each of her cheeks, her eyelids, her nose and, finally, her mouth. "We are," he said. And he kissed her again.

EPILOGUE

"THIS CELEBRATION GETS wilder every year," Delaney said. Holding hands, she and Mike walked across their backyard where a party was in full swing.

"Happy anniversary, you two." Stonewall raised his beer in toast.

"Happy tenth anniversary." Mike squeezed Delaney's hand.

She leaned in to kiss him.

"I like this," Dan called from his chair on the deck. "Ten years, three kids and still public displays of affection." He bent to kiss Megan.

Mike grinned. "The first party was the best," he said.

They'd married later that first summer, after the other weddings were over, the band shell finished, the summer concert series booked and the '57 Chevy restored and driven in the Fourth of July parade.

Once everyone learned what Aunt Ellie

had been trying to do, they all became determined to meet the terms of the will even though they didn't have to. The Henrys had even quit fighting—most of the time.

The party was a tradition now. An anniversary of their wedding, the will and the legacy left by Ellie Clark, a celebration that tied them all together.

"Hey, Dad." Andy fell into step beside them. "Can I take the car to the beach tomorrow? Everyone wants to go one more time before we head back to college."

Mike looked at Delaney.

"It's all yours, sweetie," she said. "Have fun." She watched Andy head back toward her friends. Love filled her heart and she looked at Mike. "The first was wonderful, you're right. But I think I like this one best."

"You say that every year." Mike nuzzled his wife's hair.

She nodded. "That's because every passing year reminds me that we've found happily-ever-after. And, as it turns out, that's all I ever really wanted, after all."

* * * * *

Here's a sneak peek at
THE CEO'S CHRISTMAS PROPOSITION,
the first in USA TODAY *bestselling author*
Merline Lovelace's
HOLIDAYS ABROAD *trilogy*
coming in November 2008.

American Devon McShay is about to get
the Christmas surprise of a lifetime when
she meets her new client, sexy billionaire
Caleb Logan, for the very first time.

Silhouette
Desire

Available November 2008

Her breath whistled out in a sigh of relief when he exited Customs. Devon recognized him right away from the newspaper and magazine articles her friend and partner Sabrina had looked up during her frantic prep work.

Caleb John Logan, Jr. Thirty-one. Six-two. With jet-black hair, laser-blue eyes and a linebacker's shoulders under his charcoal-gray cashmere overcoat. His jaw-dropping good looks didn't score him any points with Devon. She'd learned the hard way not to trust handsome heartbreakers like Cal Logan.

But he was a client. An important one. And

she was willing to give someone who'd served a hitch in the marines before earning a B.S. from the University of Oregon, an MBA from Stanford and his first million at the ripe old age of twenty-six the benefit of the doubt.

Right up until he spotted the hot-pink pashmina, that is.

Devon knew the flash of color was more visible than the sign she held up with his name on it. So she wasn't surprised when Logan picked her out of the crowd and cut in her direction. She'd just plastered on her best businesswoman smile when he whipped an arm around her waist. The next moment she was sprawled against his cashmere-covered chest.

"Hello, brown eyes."

Swooping down, he covered her mouth with his.

Sheer astonishment kept Devon rooted to the spot for a few seconds while her mind whirled chaotically. Her first thought was that her client had downed a few too many drinks during the long flight. Her second, that he'd mistaken the kind of escort and consulting services her company provided. Her third shoved everything else out of her head.

The man could kiss!

His mouth moved over hers with a skill that ignited sparks at a half dozen flash points throughout her body. Devon hadn't experienced that kind of spontaneous combustion in a while. A *long* while.

The sparks were still popping when she pushed off his chest, only now they fueled a flush of anger.

"Do you always greet women you don't know with a lip-lock, Mr. Logan?"

A smile crinkled the skin at the corners of his eyes. "As a matter of fact, I don't. That was from Don."

"Huh?"

"He said he owed you one from New Year's Eve two years ago and made me promise to deliver it."

She stared up at him in total incomprehension. Logan hooked a brow and attempted to prompt a nonexistent memory.

"He abandoned you at the Waldorf. Five minutes before midnight. To deliver twins."

"I don't have a clue who or what you're…"

Understanding burst like a water balloon.

"Wait a sec. Are you talking about Sabrina's old boyfriend? Your buddy, who's now an ob-gyn doc?"

It was Logan's turn to look startled. He recovered faster than Devon had, though. His smile widened into a rueful grin.

"I take it you're not Sabrina Russo."

"No, Mr. Logan, I am *not*."

* * * * *

Be sure to look for
THE CEO'S CHRISTMAS PROPOSITION
by Merline Lovelace.
Available in November 2008 wherever books
are sold, including most bookstores,
supermarkets, drugstores and
discount stores.

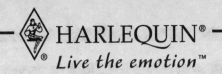

HARLEQUIN®
Live the emotion™

The series you love are now available in

LARGER PRINT!

The books are complete and unabridged—
printed in a larger type size to make it
easier on your eyes.

H A R L E Q U I N   R O M A N C E®

From the Heart, For the Heart

INTRIGUE

Breathtaking Romantic Suspense

HARLEQUIN®
Presents~

Seduction and Passion Guaranteed!

Super Romance®

Exciting, Emotional, Unexpected

Try LARGER PRINT today!

Visit: www.eHarlequin.com
Call: 1-800-873-8635

HLPDIR07

HARLEQUIN ROMANCE®

The rush of falling in love,

Cosmopolitan,
international settings,

Believable, feel-good stories
about today's women

The compelling thrill
of romantic excitement

It could happen to you!

EXPERIENCE
HARLEQUIN ROMANCE!

Available wherever Harlequin Books are sold.

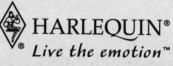

HARLEQUIN®
Live the emotion™

www.eHarlequin.com

HROMDIR04

HARLEQUIN®

American ★ *Romance*®

Invites *you* to experience
lively, heartwarming
all-American romances

Every month, we bring you four strong,
sexy men, and four women who know what
they want—and go all out to get it.

From small towns to big cities, experience
a sense of adventure, romance and family
spirit—the all-American way!

American ★ *Romance*®

Love, Home & Happiness

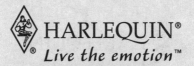
HARLEQUIN®
Live the emotion™

www.eHarlequin.com   HARDIR08

HARLEQUIN®
INTRIGUE®

BREATHTAKING ROMANTIC SUSPENSE

Shared dangers and passions lead to electrifying romance and heart-stopping suspense!

Every month, you'll meet six new heroes who are guaranteed to make your spine tingle and your pulse pound. With them you'll enter into the exciting world of Harlequin Intrigue— where your life is on the line and so is your heart!

THAT'S INTRIGUE— ROMANTIC SUSPENSE AT ITS BEST!

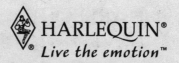

HARLEQUIN®
Live the emotion™

www.eHarlequin.com   INTDIR06

Harlequin® Historical
Historical Romantic Adventure!

Imagine a time of chivalrous
knights and unconventional ladies,
roguish rakes and impetuous
heiresses, rugged cowboys
and spirited frontierswomen—
these rich and vivid tales will
capture your imagination!

Harlequin Historical . . .
they're too good to miss!

HHDIR06

HARLEQUIN®
Presents~

The world's bestselling romance series...
The series that brings you your favorite authors,
month after month:

Helen Bianchin...Emma Darcy
Lynne Graham...Penny Jordan
Miranda Lee...Sandra Marton
Anne Mather...Carole Mortimer
Melanie Milburne...Michelle Reid

and many more talented authors!

Wealthy, powerful, gorgeous men...
Women who have feelings just like your own...
The stories you love, set in exotic, glamorous locations...

HARLEQUIN®
Presents~

Seduction and Passion Guaranteed!

HPDIR08

www.eHarlequin.com